He reached for her hand, but she couldn't stand his touch

"Don't. I only want to feel my baby." Lydia laid her hand on her stomach, aching to feel the sensation of their unborn son, lazily twisting inside her. "I miss him."

Josh's expression went blank again. He folded his hands, white-knuckled, in his lap.

She could end it now, put a stop to the loneliness and fear. Once they'd married, he'd considered their relationship complete, nothing more to worry about. He'd turned his attention to his priorities—his clients. Feeling left out and unneeded, more hurt than she'd ever admitted, she'd tried arguing, explaining, and finally she'd found poor comfort in her own work. But the baby had made them try again.

She had two choices. Tear him to shreds or try to save their marriage. Could hurting him ever be revenge enough?

Dear Reader,

My favorite romances are about couples struggling with life—the everyday challenges that follow that first happily ever after. It can be small things—not knowing your mate prefers potatoes when you love rice, needing the comfort of a thin sliver of night-light when he can sleep only in total darkness and complete silence. Or it could be, as with Lydia and Josh Quincy, separate views of life that simply refuse to meld.

Josh and Lydia coast along in their marriage, ignoring ever-increasing differences, until a tragedy forces them to reevaluate everything about themselves—what they want, where they want to live, if they can be together. Even in the best of marriages, these questions arise, and I'm always curious about how we answer them. Josh and Lydia made me wonder how I'd answer them myself.

I hope you'll enjoy this story, which remains with me still. I'd love to hear from you. Please feel free to e-mail me at anna@annaadams.net.

Best wishes,

Anna

MARRIAGE IN JEOPARDY

Anna Adams

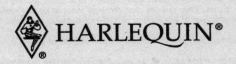

HARLEQUIN®

TORONTO • NEW YORK • LONDON
AMSTERDAM • PARIS • SYDNEY • HAMBURG
STOCKHOLM • ATHENS • TOKYO • MILAN • MADRID
PRAGUE • WARSAW • BUDAPEST • AUCKLAND

ISBN 0-373-71336-3

MARRIAGE IN JEOPARDY

Printed in U.S.A.

Books by Anna Adams

HARLEQUIN SUPERROMANCE

Don't miss any of our special offers. Write to us at the
following address for information on our newest releases.

Harlequin Reader Service
U.S.: 3010 Walden Ave., P.O. Box 1325, Buffalo, NY 14269
Canadian: P.O. Box 609, Fort Erie, Ont. L2A 5X3

To Sarah—with all my love and my deepest hopes that all you desire and dream of will come to you. You are the essence of joy. You shine with hope. You make me glad.

CHAPTER ONE

LYDIA QUINCY OPENED her eyes. Memory rushed at her with the menace of an oncoming tornado. She remembered walking out of the elevator at the courthouse construction site. A woman had come around a stack of bricks. She'd never forget that woman's mouth, stretched in a grin of pure malice. Lydia's muscles clenched as she tried to duck again. That woman had swung a piece of rebar straight into Lydia's stomach.

The moment replayed like a loop of film.

She tried to breathe.

Staring around the unfamiliar room, she saw blank tan walls and mountains of hoses, wires, tubing. A machine that screamed with blinking numbers. A shapeless beige curtain and hard plastic rails on her bed.

One more breath brought nausea so strong she had to escape. She struggled to sit, but an IV stung her arm. Oxygen tubing pulled her head back.

"Lydia?" Evelyn, her mother-in-law, spoke to her in a sleepy voice. How could she be here? She lived four hours away. "Lie down, honey." Evelyn leapt to her feet, sending a metal chair screeching across the tile floor.

Lydia slumped against a flat pillow and it crackled beneath her head. She pushed both hands down to her stomach, but bone deep, she already knew what had happened.

The physical pain was nothing, compared to her grief. She drew her knees high, clamping her hands to her belly. She felt only emptiness. Not life. Emptiness.

"My baby." She let her hands sink to her sides. "My baby," she cried in anguish more animal than human.

Evelyn grabbed her arm. Tears washed her glasses and spilled over her lined cheeks.

"I'm sorry." She peered toward the door, as if she hoped someone would show up and save her.

"Where's Josh?" Lydia half expected he'd stayed at work.

Evelyn had been reaching for the call button at Lydia's side, but drew back. "He wanted to be the one to tell you, but I can explain—"

"I know. Don't say it out loud." The second someone did, her pregnancy would be truly over.

All that hope, so futile now… She couldn't stop loving her son just because she'd never have him.

"Lydia, honey…"

She pushed at her mother-in-law's thin shoulders. "No, no, no."

"Shh," Evelyn whispered, putting her arms around Lydia anyway. "Shh."

Lydia sobbed. *"I want my baby."* He'd died, but somehow she hadn't. "Why am I alive?"

Evelyn moved away, grimacing. "I know how you feel, but you can't—you have to live."

A nurse hurried into the room and nudged Evelyn away. "Mrs. Quincy, I'm glad you're awake." The woman checked the machine's readouts and threaded the IV tubes through her fingers. "Mrs. Quincy?" she repeated as if she needed Lydia to answer.

"I'm all right." Lydia nodded at the nurse, but reached for her mother-in-law. Her hand fell through air to the sheets. "Is Josh in court? How did you get here first, Evelyn, when his office is only a few blocks away?"

"Your husband?" the nurse asked. "He's here. He passed our station a few minutes ago."

"He left?" Typical, but still it hurt. Things had begun to get better during the twenty-two weeks of her pregnancy, but before then, they'd spent much of their five-year marriage pulling in opposite directions, unable to speak, unable to explain why they couldn't. Once they'd learned the baby was coming, they'd both wanted him so much they'd pretended nothing was wrong.

"Josh has been here whenever they let us in," Evelyn defended her son. "But you know how he is. Impatience and anger go hand in hand, and add worrying about you—he needed a walk."

Lydia knew Josh better than his mother did. While she could hardly hear above the pain screaming in her own head, Josh had no doubt taken refuge in calls to his office. That was Josh. If he couldn't fix his private life, he turned to maintaining his reputation as the best public defender in Hartford, Connecticut.

"I—" She wanted to be angry. God knew, she'd had practice, but she needed her husband. He'd lost their baby, too.

"What?" Evelyn asked. "What can I do for you?"

"Do?" No one could erase the instant or the memory. Sun glinting off a green truck's hood had blinded her as she'd walked around the bricks. One of those bricks had grazed her arm. She turned her elbow, trying to see the scrape, to see anything except that woman.

Her unborn son had probably died the moment the rebar hit. She covered her mouth.

"Try not to think about what happened. Let me call Josh."

"Don't go." She didn't trust herself to think on her own yet.

Evelyn squeezed her hand but turned to the nurse. "My daughter-in-law's lips are cracking. Can you get her something?" Her voice rasped as if she'd been yelling.

"How long have you been here?" Lydia had assumed this was the same day, but her mother-in-law looked tired and worn.

"I'll bring you both something to drink." The nurse gave the machines a last look as she backed toward the door. "Mrs. Quincy, you're in good shape. Your doctor will be in to see you—well, I can't say for sure when—but you don't need to worry."

Not worry? She had to be nuts.

"What happened after she hit me, Evelyn?"

Josh's mother splayed her fingers into short red curls that were flat on one side from her long stint in the chair. "I'll tell you what we know." Weariness veined her eyes. She stole a glance at her watch. "Unless you want me to find Josh," she said again.

This woman who never cried on the principle that tears were weakness had cried a lot. Lydia brushed a teardrop off her own cheek.

"He's not here. Explain what happened to my baby. I remember being at the courthouse." An architect, she'd been hired to help restore it to eighteenth-century splendor. She'd visited that day only to discuss a change with the contractor. "I was leaving." At a new wave of sorrow, she pressed her palms to her stomach again. "How long have I been here?" How many days had she been alive instead of her son, who'd never had a chance to live?

"Three days." Evelyn wiped her face with the hem of her cotton shirt. "You've been awake now and then."

"I don't remember." But bursts of pain and light and that damn machine bleating ran through her mind. "Who was she?"

"Vivian Durance. I lost her husband's case." Josh's voice, thick with sorrow, made Lydia and Evelyn look toward the doorway. He stood, frozen.

His words didn't register. She drank him in, desperate, because he was the only one who could really understand. Tall and aloof-looking—as always, when he felt most emotional—he stared at her, guilt in his brown-black eyes. Tight dark curls stood on end as if he'd yanked at his hair to punish himself.

"I'll wait outside," Evelyn said, and she passed Josh without looking at him.

He stepped aside to avoid his mother's touch.

After the door closed, he crossed to the bed, unsure of his welcome. Lydia held out her arms. With a sigh, his eyes beginning to redden, he caught her, his arms rough. She flinched.

"I'm sorry." He eased up a little, but when he buried his face in her shoulder, his breathing was jagged. "I'm sorry."

His remorse forced the truth to sink in. "Vivian Durance is married to one of your clients?"

She'd been afraid of this, a low-grade fear, like a fever she'd never managed to get over. About two weeks after their wedding, the first threat from an unsatisfied client had arrived in the form of red paint thrown across their town house's door. The client's father had also slipped a red-stained note through the letter box. "If my son goes to prison, you die," it read, and it was written with so much rage, the words almost ripped the paper.

Josh had repainted the door, chucked the note away and reassured her that all attorneys, even public defenders, occasionally received threats. Two years later another client had met him on the courthouse steps. Everyone who'd seen the man on the stand knew his own testimony had sealed a guilty verdict. Nevertheless, the man had blamed Josh, screaming until the cops had dragged him away.

Three more years had passed, but Lydia had never again felt entirely safe.

"Did you know she was coming after us? What did she say to you?" Lydia tried not to blame him, but the words begged to be said.

"Nothing." He leaned back. "She screamed at the court in general."

"What aren't you telling me?"

He shook his head, but his eyes were blank. He was hiding something.

Furiously, she bit down on the words, but she couldn't help herself. "Third time's the charm, I guess. Someone finally got to us."

"That's what I was afraid of," he said, his calm dignified—and infuriating. "That you'd blame me."

"Our baby didn't have to die."

"I am sorry." His lips barely moved. She'd loved his mouth, full, moist, capable of giving her pleasure that was almost pain. That was the physical part of their marriage. Nothing else about living together had come easy. "I'm not hiding anything," he said. "The truth was bad enough."

She stared, unable to speak. He was in shock, too, which exaggerated his guilt. It couldn't be all his fault.

"I lost Carter Durance's capital case. After the

police caught her, Vivian said she felt someone I loved needed to die, too." Josh stated the facts without defending himself. "I tried everything I could think of to save the man, but he wasn't crazy or innocent enough."

Lydia pushed her fists into her eyes. His flat tone hurt most of all.

"Lydia?" He'd said her name a million times, but never before had it sounded like begging.

"I have nothing more to give." This Vivian had taken everything. "Why do you have to defend guilty people?"

Pain rippled across his face. "You know why. Almost everyone I defend grew up the way I did. I made better choices, but do you know how many times I see myself and my parents in my clients?"

She didn't answer. He hadn't mentioned his sister. Clara was the one he couldn't stop trying to save. She'd drowned in the family's filthy swimming pool while his parents had lain unconscious, too drunk to know they were alive, much less that their daughter had died.

Josh couldn't forgive his parents or himself, though he'd been at school when it had happened. Now he was compelled to rescue all the poor, defenseless Claras.

"You aren't like them," she said. "You'll never

drink the way your parents did. You can stop serving penance." She wrapped her arms around her waist. "I deserved better and so did our baby."

"Wait." He tried to cradle her chin, but she turned her head, and he flinched as if she'd hit him. "Some of my clients are innocent. Even the guilty ones have rights, but I'd have dumped Carter Durance if I'd known this might happen." Emotion flooded his voice. "I'd never risk our child."

Her own anguish, reflected in his broken tone, confused her.

He reached for her hand this time, but she couldn't stand his touch. "Don't. I only want to feel my baby." She laid her hand on her stomach, aching to feel the sensation of their unborn son, lazily twisting inside her. "I miss him."

Josh's expression went blank again. He folded his hands, white-knuckled, in his lap.

She could end it now, put a stop to the loneliness and fear. Once they'd married, he'd considered their relationship complete, nothing more to worry about. He'd turned his attention to his priorities—his clients. Feeling left out and unneeded, more hurt than she'd ever admitted, she'd tried arguing, explaining, and finally, she'd found poor comfort in her own work. But the baby had made them both try.

"I'm sorry."

She had two choices. Tear him to shreds or try to save their marriage. Could hurting him ever be revenge enough? And how could she ignore his grief, as harrowing as her own?

"I couldn't save him, either," she said, choosing marriage. "Moms are supposed to protect their babies."

He flexed his hands. "I'd give anything to have him safe and you unhurt."

His bleakness affected her. Maybe her feelings for Josh had never been sane. Too intense, too much passion at first. Neither of them had fully considered what came after "I do."

"We can't bring him back, but we don't have to keep hurting each other. I know I made mistakes, too." She couldn't look at him.

"We can stop making them."

She might not be ready to give up on her marriage, but total forgiveness didn't come easily. She couldn't forget how hard she'd tried to make him care about his home life as much as he cared about work. "What do we have now?" She wiped her cheeks.

Josh held her against him. "You have me." The strain in his corded arms reminded her of more tender moments when she'd loved him so much she could hardly breathe. "He was my baby, too."

No attempt to explain—no defense, just desolation. His whisper, rich with sorrow, pulled her back to him.

A WEEK AFTER Lydia had awakened, Josh stopped at his wife's door, feeling as if today was their final connection with their son. She'd lost the baby the day of the attack, and they'd dealt with her D&C and with the police questioning her about her few memories. When they left the hospital, everything about her pregnancy would be over.

He pressed his fist to Lydia's door, glancing at the busy nurses, the visitors striding up and down the beige-tiled hall. Their lives went on.

And he wanted to hit someone.

"Who's out there?"

Lydia sounded scared. He shoved the door open. Of course she'd be afraid one of the Durances would come back to finish the job.

"Hi." He plastered on a smile and held out a cellophane-wrapped bunch of wildflowers he'd picked up in the lobby.

After staring at them as if she didn't understand, she popped the top off her oversize drinking cup. "Thanks. Want to put them in water?"

"You don't plan to be thirsty again?"

She shrugged, her distant gaze telling him she

was submerged in her own grief. He unwrapped the flowers and pushed the stems into the cup.

"I like them," she said.

He brushed his lips across her temple and took the cup to the bathroom to add more water. When he set it back on the table, the scrape of plastic across laminate seemed to awaken her.

"Do me a favor?" She turned her breakfast tray toward him.

"Anything," he said, putting desperation before common sense.

She pointed to the bland scrambled eggs and a bowl of oatmeal. A piece of toast with one bite out of it lay across the plate's pale green lip. "Finish this. They won't let me go if I'm not eating, and I can't force it down."

She touched her stomach, but quickly dragged her hand away. They both looked anywhere except at each other. Funny the things that reminded you.

"You need nourishment." Man, he sounded like a granny. He glanced toward the door. "I can't do something that's bad for you."

"If I have to fly through that window, I'm getting out of here today, but I'm too tired for the argument." She nudged the tray again. "Is it because of your oatmeal thing?"

His "oatmeal thing" was a hatred for the stuff. "It's my wanting-you-to-be-well thing."

Her sharp glance suggested he didn't have the right, but she glossed over the moment. "Eat this stuff for me, and I'll devour anything else later."

He dug into the congealed paste—oatmeal—and washed each bite down with cold eggs, stopping only to gag. When Lydia smiled, even oatmeal was worth it.

"What's it like at home, Josh?"

Empty. Grim.

He looked for something to drink. How much damage could those flowers do to a cup of water? A coffee cup sat empty on the table just beyond her tray.

"What do you mean?" If he told her the truth, would she refuse to come home? A hug and the grief they'd shared the other day hadn't put them on stable ground.

"Knowing it's just you and me from now on."

"I should have taken the nursery apart." Neither of them needed reminders of how they'd painted and decorated and argued over the right way to assemble the changing table and bed.

"No," she said. "I want to be the one who puts his things away."

She blamed him so much she seemed to think he

had no rights where his own child was concerned. "We'll do it together." He choked down another bite of oatmeal. She didn't answer. In her eyes, he saw all the unanswered questions between them. "Unless you don't want us to do anything together."

She lowered her head.

"No?" he asked. The oatmeal almost came back up.

She shook her hair out of her eyes. "If not for the baby, we'd have split up months ago. I need to be sure you want to go on, too."

He'd felt this kind of shock three times—when Clara had died, when the hospital had called him about Lydia and now. "You would have left me?"

Her mouth twisted with bitterness that seemed totally out of character for Lydia. "We'd have left each other," she said. "Who cares who would have packed first?"

She must be out of her— "Are you crazy? I married you for better or worse. I'm not leaving you."

"Why?" With no makeup and no pretense, she looked naked. "You don't love me anymore."

"Not love you? Have we been sharing the same bed?"

"I'm not talking about sex," she said—loudly enough to make him glance toward the door.

"You're the one who changed. You can't—" How could he put his humiliation into words? "Can't stand to let me hold you. Can't let me touch you. Can't let me kiss you."

"I can't stand the silence," she said. "It was bad enough before, but all I want now is the baby."

He didn't pretend he'd been happy with their relationship, either. "It was getting better," he said. "I thought we seemed closer again."

"You mean we spoke once or twice at night if you got home before I went to bed, or if I called you from my office? We shared a chaste kiss before the lights went out and sex on the weekend if you found time away from the law library."

How many times had she rolled away from him? "You didn't want—"

"Yeah—right." Her sarcasm left him cold. "And I just couldn't tear myself away from work, either."

"I thought you were excited about your projects." Not always, he realized now. He'd wondered….

She stared at him, a hard, emotionless woman he'd never met and couldn't hope to know. "Are you that insensitive?"

"I must be. Are you saying you want a divorce?"

She pulled her knees all the way to her chest, grimacing. Hunched over, she looked defeated. "I thought I could go on the other day, when I woke up, but now, I don't know."

He wanted to grab her so she couldn't push him away. "I don't even like going home now," he said. She shot him another accusing glance, as if, like her, he missed only the baby. He shook his head. "I miss you, Lydia. I want you back."

A frown lined her forehead.

"Why didn't you tell me you were that unhappy?"

She linked her fingers at her ankles. "You stopped caring. I tried to tell you, but you never heard. Your job makes you happy, and I don't."

She'd left him room to fight. "I like my job, but you're my wife. Just talk to me when you're worried about something as crazy as my not caring."

"Why should I have to tell you? A woman shouldn't have to ask her husband—*I* shouldn't have had to beg you to notice me."

Defensive—and upset—he apparently didn't know how to fight after all. "What do you need?"

She stretched out her legs and smoothed the sheet across her breasts. "I was serious about the third time being the charm. Three threats in five years shouldn't seem so frightening, but that woman killed our family. I won't ever forget."

"You want me to quit?"

"Would you?"

"I don't think I can." He'd had one goal since college—to make people who'd grown up the way he had see that they could choose something cleaner, safer. He worked like hell to keep them out of jail and show them they didn't have to repeat their parents' mistakes. They didn't have to give their children dangerous lives. They could keep their families out of the system that had let him down. He cared about those people who were as faceless and nameless as he'd been when his parents had gone to prison for neglecting his sister.

"Lydia, I can't stop. What would I do?"

Tears filled her eyes. She fingered them away. "I'm afraid that if you can't change, I will. I've thought about this all night. We're about to go home, and I'm not sure there's a reason to go together."

"Nothing like this will happen again. It was an aberration."

"It won't ever happen to me again."

CHAPTER TWO

"MR. QUINCY, if you'll bring your car to the front entrance, we'll take Lydia down." Patty, Lydia's nurse, took her bag of belongings and passed it, along with the cup of flowers, to Josh. "We'll meet you at the doors."

Josh looked at Lydia, longing in his eyes. They'd finished a wary morning. He'd gathered her things, talked about dinner tonight, assumed they were going home together.

"Are you all right?" he asked, but she knew he was asking if she'd rather call a cab.

She hesitated. She couldn't turn back again. This time, it was give up or give in. "I'm fine."

After he turned the corner, Patty put on her reading glasses and peered through several sheets of paper. "Let me see." She ran her index finger down the print. "Watch for a rise in temperature and extra sensitivity in your abdominal region that might indicate internal bleeding. No sexual relations for six weeks."

"No—" She'd almost said "no problem," but stopped just in time to avoid flinging her dirty laundry at Patty's feet.

"These are the numbers for the nurse's desk and for Dr. Sprague. Call if you have any questions." Patty took off her specs. "I'm working Monday, Wednesday and Friday from eight until eight."

Unexpectedly warmed by an almost-stranger's concern, Lydia smiled.

"I'd like to hear how you're getting along."

"I'll call."

"Okay." Patty looked up as an orderly pushed a squeaking wheelchair into the room. "Shall we?"

Lydia sat and folded her hands to hide their shaking. The town house hadn't felt like home since she'd first begun to think about leaving Josh, but if she was starting over she had to go home.

The trip in the small blue-gray elevator went too quickly. As the doors opened, a cool gust of air blew in. Lydia breathed deep. The orderly pushed her past a long row of wide windows and delivered her to the sidewalk as Josh pulled up in their car.

"Thanks," Lydia said to the man behind her, though she avoided his helping hands as she stood.

"You're welcome," he said. "Best of luck." He nodded to Josh and went back inside.

"Are you in pain?" Josh opened the passenger's door.

She shook her head and let her hair blow across her face. She assumed his tenderness, as he eased her into the seat, was for the baby they weren't taking home. He pulled her seat belt out, but she fastened it herself. "Thanks," she said.

"I'll take it easy."

The bumps in the road didn't matter. Neither did the stab of pain in her belly when Josh had to slam on the brakes for a VW bug whose driver sped through a red light.

"Damn it!" His ferocity had nothing to do with the bug's driver.

"Can we stop?" She risked her first look at him since they'd left. "I don't want to go home. I thought I could do it, but…"

He was clenching his jaw so hard she wouldn't have been surprised to hear his teeth shatter. He glanced into the rearview mirror and then checked over his shoulder and pulled to the curb. "Where do you want me to take you?"

She glanced into the backseat. She didn't even have a sweater. "Nowhere's practical."

"Then come home and think about what you're doing."

"I was trying to, but it doesn't feel like home."

He nodded, a brief jab of his chin in the air. She didn't blame him.

"I'm not trying to hurt you on purpose. I just don't know how to pretend anymore."

"And you can't make up your mind?"

She looked out at the passing traffic, at the sun that seemed too bright for a day like this, and at a couple strolling by with their young daughter holding their hands.

"I'm panicking." She wiped sweat from beneath her bangs. "But I want to be with you. I mean that."

"Trust me."

"If it were that easy, we wouldn't be talking about this at all." She folded her hands in her lap and glanced over her shoulder. "Let's go. I'm all right. I won't do this again."

"Maybe you shouldn't promise that."

She searched his face for sarcasm but found only compassion. It made a huge difference because fear was driving her, and he had a right to be angry. A chip fell out of her massive store of resentment.

Still, she clung to the sides of her seat when he parked in front of the town house. "I'm glad none of the neighbors are out."

He nodded and pulled the keys from the ignition. "They mean well, but I don't know what to say when they tell me they're sorry."

They both got out of the car. Lydia planted her fists in the small of her back and stared at the wreath on their door, the open drapes she hadn't been home to close. The baby's nursery was on the second floor. She walked up the sidewalk as fast as her aching body would let her to avoid looking at that window.

EVELYN STARED at the white phone that hung on her white kitchen wall.

"I should call him."

"He won't feel better if you do."

She jumped. "Bart, I didn't know you were home." Turning, she crossed the kitchen to take her husband's coat and hang it on one of the pegs in the mudroom.

He took off his boots and stared at them. "I forgot to change when I got off the boat."

"Put them in the bench. If we can't stand the smell of our own lobster and fish and ocean water by now…" She didn't know how to end that sentence. "It doesn't matter. You really think Josh wouldn't want me to call? Isn't this different?"

"To us. Not to him."

"We were supposed to have a grandchild." A grandchild that might have brought Josh back to them.

Bart pulled her close and kissed her forehead. Usually that made her feel better. "For all we know, it's brought back memories of Clara and he hates us more than ever."

"You can't blame him." She wiped her mouth. Eighteen years since she'd had her last drink, but the thirst could still bring her to her knees. She stepped away from Bart and went to the sink, grateful for dirty lunch dishes. She started running the water and slid her hands beneath its warmth.

"If you want to call him that badly, maybe you should." Bart gripped her upper arms for a minute and then let go. "I just hate that you have to prepare yourself to be hurt."

"He might understand. He's lost a child, too." She thought of Clara. Rather, a memory of Clara stole into her mind. Her baby, in pink shorts that bagged almost to her knees, brown hair blowing across her eyes and a spade almost as tall as she was for digging in the sand.

Evelyn clenched her eyes shut and willed that wisp of memory to leave. She didn't deserve to remember the good times, and the worst day was just a nightmare feeling she could call to mind.

She'd been so drunk she only knew what had happened after her daughter had died.

"Josh didn't lose his child the way we did." Bart started toward the hallway. "I'll wash up. You do what you have to, Evelyn."

"Bart—"

He stopped. She wrapped her wet arms around him, finding his sea scents comfortingly familiar. "Thanks," she said. "I'm tired of him pushing us away. But how can we complain? He raised himself. He was more father and mother to Clara than we were."

"Not just because of you." He looked backward in time. "The catches were so sparse. I was afraid I couldn't feed you all. I've asked myself the same question since the day Clara… Why didn't I work harder, instead of drinking harder?"

"And why couldn't I want to be a mom?" Evelyn made herself say the words, each one like hammering a nail in her own coffin. Josh had been a total surprise to her and Bart. She'd wanted to be a teacher, but pregnant at nineteen, she'd dropped out of college. As a mom, she was a total misfit, never feeling the instincts that came naturally to other women.

She'd thought something was wrong with her colicky son, but no matter how many times she'd dragged Josh to the doctor, they just kept telling her he was fine—healthy—and she'd get used to motherhood. She'd tried some of Bart's vodka one night, just after she'd put her baby to bed. The vodka had eased her pain.

Finally, it had numbed her.

She pulled Bart even closer. "I might have been better with their baby."

"It wouldn't matter. You think Josh would have let us see him?"

"He's not cruel. He's sad. We have to stick it out—if only because Josh feels as guilty about Clara as we do." It was only after the state had put her and Bart in jail for eighteen months for negligence that she'd learned not to give up trying to be a good mother.

"*He* has no reason to feel guilty."

"If he could believe that, maybe he'd learn to forgive us and be our son again. And I wonder if something's wrong between him and Lydia. Even when they're together, they— I feel distance between them."

"What are you talking about, Evelyn?" He let her go and turned off the water just before it reached the top of the sink.

"If you disagreed with me, you'd say so. You've been worried, too." She dunked the dishes into the sink, taking comfort from the clash of glass and stoneware. "It's time we stopped just waiting for things to get better," she said. "I'm going to ask them to come up here."

Bart took the first plate she handed him. Even filthy from working on the boat, he started drying. It was habit. She washed. He dried. People with addictive, alcoholic personalities found strength in habits.

"Lydia might come. Josh won't." He set the plate down and then stared at his dirty jeans. "I'm stinking up the place. Let me shower and I'll help you."

"I'm fine. Go ahead." She set a plate in the other half of the sink, her mind on her spiel to Josh. How could she convince him to come home and get over his sadness?

So aware of her thoughts after thirty-three years together, Bart stopped and said, "Listen to me, Evelyn." His anxiety came through.

"He may turn me down, but how do you think Lydia feels in that house, with the nursery down the hall? Josh will come if he thinks it'll help her."

"Lydia loves us, but her loyalty belongs to him. She won't come up here, knowing Josh can't stand to be in this house."

Evelyn turned. She put her hands on her hips,

not caring when a marshmallow cloud of dish-washing suds dropped to the floor. "You forget—you can slide along, think you're doing all right—but when you lose a child, nothing is ever the same. Lydia loves Josh, but she'll be hating that room."

They had a room of their own, hardly opened in the past eighteen years, still filled with Clara's things. If she could have cut that room out of her house, she would have dropped it over the cliffs on the headland. And yet—it was all she had left of her daughter.

"You'd use Lydia?" Bart didn't like that.

She struggled with a surge of guilt. "Use her, yes." She couldn't pretend to be better than she was. "But I love her as if she were ours. She needs a mother and father as much as Josh does, and I want my son back. This family has lost enough, and I'm through waiting for him to come home."

"You worry me, Evelyn."

"We've tried to give him time to make up his mind." She went back to the sink. "We've done enough penance. He'll either cut us off or we'll convince him at last that he can depend on us."

"I don't want him to cut us off," Bart said.

"This half life of having him come around once or twice a year is good enough for you?"

"It's what we have." Bart opened the fridge. He studied the bottles of water and juice and then slammed the door shut. "It's what we made."

She started washing again. Bart, loving her, even after what they'd done, had saved her life. Was she about to risk losing him, too? "We can make something better."

WRAPPED IN A pale yellow chenille blanket, Lydia stared at the evening paper, oblivious to the words. Josh came into the family room and set a cup of coffee beside her.

"Thanks." She'd craved it. He'd brewed it.

He tucked the blanket around her feet. She tried not to move away from his hands.

Somehow, he knew. He looked at her with the knowledge of her instinctive rejection in his eyes. "Should you go to bed?" he asked.

"I don't know. They just told me to call if I felt bad." She hunched her shoulders and cupped her mug in both hands. The coffee should have been too hot, but it warmed her against a cold that came from deep inside.

"If you're staying down here, I'll start a fire."

She glanced toward the fireplace. Gray ash and small black chunks crowded the hearth. The familiar scent of apple and wood smoke usually comforted her. "Okay, but then sit for a while. You don't have to do anything else for me."

Surprise made him look at her. "You want to talk?"

"I'd just like knowing you're near." She had to believe he wasn't thinking up ways to get back to the office.

Nodding, he began to scoop the ashes into an old-fashioned coal scuttle they'd found in a shop in his hometown in Maine. No polished copper affair, this was a dusty, dented black metal working scuttle. Like their marriage, it had taken a beating. "Something's on your mind," he said.

She glanced at the phone, resting beside a stack of her library books on a table beneath the bay window. "I promised your mother I'd call when we got home."

He opened his mouth, then shut it.

She'd seen his parents through his eyes at first. Alcoholics, who'd thrown his childhood down the neck of a vodka bottle. But he'd never given them credit for cleaning up after Clara's death.

"They love us," she said. "Both of us." He didn't seem to need his parents' love.

"I don't want to talk to them."

"Okay. Josh?"

He stopped, midway across the room. A vein

stood out on his forearm as his knuckles whitened around the bucket's handle.

"Sometimes I wonder what I'd have to do to make you as angry with me."

"As angry?"

"As you are with your parents."

"Are you looking for an argument?"

"No." But she was tired of trying to keep the peace. "I don't know."

"I get that you don't want to be here."

She couldn't control a shiver as she thought of the nursery and their bedroom. She hadn't forced herself to climb the stairs yet. Too many memories waited up there. "Listen." She willed him to understand how the nothingness pressed in on her. "Don't you hear the silence? I know you mean well, but all the fires and blankets and warm drinks in the world won't help. I'm afraid to say anything because I'm hurt. And I'm afraid your mind is at the office."

"What do you want?" Long and lean and unreachable, he went to the door. "I'm trying. I don't want to lose you, but I can't quit my job and sell this house today." He glanced at the ceiling. "I feel that room, too, but this is our home. I want to learn to live with the empty nursery and your anger and my—" He paused, shaking his head. "My fear," he said. "That you're going to leave me because it's my fault our baby died."

"Let's do something," Lydia said. "Let's get out of here, spend some time somewhere else, just the two of us."

"And then come back to the problems you say we've ignored for years?"

The phone rang. A frown crossed his face. He picked up the receiver and scanned the caller ID. Then he crossed the room and handed it to her. "I don't want to talk to them," he said.

His parents. She clicked the talk button as Josh took the bucket out. "Evelyn?"

"How are you? Is Josh all right?"

"I'm fine. He's quiet."

"How quiet? You have to make him talk."

Or he'd retreat from her as he had from Evelyn and Bart? "We're settling back in."

"Come up here instead."

Lydia knew she should say no. Josh couldn't talk to his mother and father. He'd refuse to see them. "I'm tired. Staying here might be—"

"Come tomorrow, then. You don't want to be in that house right now. Let me pamper you and make sure you're taking care of yourself. Let me have a daughter for a week or two."

Her voice broke on the final plea. Lydia's tears,

never far away, thickened in her throat. "I want to, but you know how things are, Evelyn."

"Josh will come if you do. Don't give him a choice for once."

Lydia laughed, as convincingly as she was able. "You wouldn't take advantage of me to soften Josh?"

"I guess I would." Evelyn was always truthful. "But I only left the hospital because I knew he didn't want me there. I've worried about you. Come let me look after you."

"Josh is taking great care of me." Lydia jumped to his defense.

"I'm saying Josh may not tuck you in, or make sure you have nice clean sheets warm from the dryer."

"I'm not taking to my bed." But such loving concern tempted her.

"And Josh won't bring you lobster fresh out of the trap. Bart will bring enough for both of you. Come, Lydia. And bring our son. Families should be together when they're hurting."

Lydia licked her lips. It was not a perfect answer, but she couldn't stand this house. She dreaded sleeping in her own bed, seeing the baby clothes stacked on the end of her dresser, the copy of *What to Expect When You're Expecting* on her nightstand. "I can't do that to Josh."

"Ask him."

"It's not right." And if she asked and he said no, she'd resent him for not seeing how much she needed to be away.

"I understand, but when do you think our family should try to love each other?"

Lydia splayed her fingers across her belly. All her hopes had died, and raising them was proving difficult. "I'm sorry, Evelyn. I can't answer you."

JOSH EMPTIED the ashes into the garbage can behind the door to their walkout basement. He gathered a couple logs from the pile beside the fence. But then he couldn't make himself go inside. As long as he stayed out here, he had an excuse to avoid talking to his parents.

Ridiculous. Childish.

He didn't care. His guilt over losing his unborn son hurt enough, but it had also opened the lid on his guilt about Clara. He should have found a way to keep her safe when he couldn't be home. It hadn't been normal for a high school freshman to take all responsibility for his five-year-old sister, but he hadn't had a choice.

He turned his attention to the dead plants in the small yard. He put down the logs. Halloween was in two days, and the cool weather was upon them.

Usually, he and Lydia had cleared out her summer garden by now, but purple and blue flowers had spread as far as the gray-brown plants the frost had already killed.

"Josh?"

He turned, a couple of withered begonias in his grasp. She stood in the doorway, her hands braced on the frame.

"You should stay away from those stairs. They're too narrow and you're not steady on your feet."

"I'm all right." She'd never accepted help or advice with enthusiasm. "What are you doing?"

"Yard work." He yanked another brown, crumbling shrub out of the ground.

"You can come in now. Your mother hung up."

"Did she ask you to go to Maine?"

Lydia widened her eyes. "How did you know?"

"Know my mother?"

Lydia let that question lie. "She asked us both, but I told her you wouldn't want to."

Another plant gave up its grip on the ground. "You were right."

"So we stay here."

"Where you don't want to be."

She started to turn away, but hesitated, distraction on her face. She loved his parents. If not for him, she'd have jumped at the chance to visit Maine.

He reached blindly for a shrub, breathing in as he got a handful of sharp holly leaves.

Lydia went to him and opened his palm. "Are you all right?"

Not with her scent wafting off the top of her head as she peered at the drops of blood on his hand.

"What were you thinking?" She blotted his palm with the hem of her sweatshirt. Grateful for her tenderness, he didn't have the strength to stop her.

"I'm realizing my parents will come between us some day."

She froze. "Come inside and let's clean that with something sterile."

"They will, won't they, Lydia? You'd rather be with my mother than with me right now. And my father's always ready to ply you with lobster."

"I was an only child. My parents are dead. Your mother and father have showered me with all the love you won't let them give you."

"Because of what they did to Clara."

"And what you think you did?" The moment the words left her mouth, she stepped back.

He paused. "How long have you been thinking that?"

"Forever. I never had the courage to suggest you're wasting your life and your parents' love

because you're afraid you caused Clara's death."
She wrapped her arms around her waist. Her
sweatshirt billowed beneath them. Her unhappi-
ness was easy to feel. "You did everything you
could for Clara and your parents have paid their
dues—in prison and in trying to win you back.
Why throw away the kind of affection you wanted
for yourself and your sister?"

"Because it's too late." He turned her, concentrating on keeping his hands light on her shoulders.
"And I have no right if Clara can't feel it, too."

"That's nuts, Josh."

He urged her through the doorway, picked up
the logs and shut the cold behind them. "I know.
I can't help it."

TWO TRUCE-FILLED DAYS brought them to Halloween. Josh finished decorating the yard about noon
and then found Lydia, dusting the little breakable
things in her mother's china cabinet. They'd hardly
ever used the formal dining room. It must have felt
safe to her, free of memories.

"What's up?" He eased a plate out of her hands.
"Did the doctor have cleaning in mind when they
told you to take it easy?"

"I can't sit still any more than you can."

Understanding, he handed the plate back. "I'd

better pick up some candy. You want anything from the grocery store?"

"I already bought some." She shot an uneasy glance at the ceiling. "It's in the nursery."

Which neither of them had entered since she'd come home. "Okay." If not for Lydia as a witness, he'd leave the candy in those bags and buy new. "I'll get it."

She braced herself, a heroine facing execution in one of those old movies she liked so much. "I'll come with you."

"I appreciate the offer, but I'll do it. One of us has to tackle that room, and I can't face another shrine."

She nodded, empathy in her eyes. "I finally understand why no one goes in Clara's room."

Josh climbed the stairs. He was starting to hate his own home. He stood in front of the door he'd closed that first night when the town house had bounced emptiness from every wall.

Treat it like a Band-Aid. Yank it off. He grabbed the doorknob and walked inside. Like a man gasping his last breath, he went to the changing table. Two shopping bags, each filled with diapers and two huge sacks of candy, sat on the plastic surface that smelled new. Unused. They wouldn't even have memories of their child.

Josh snatched at the candy and turned. Only

to face the crib. Where his son would have slept in a few more months. Where his child would never sleep now.

He stumbled. The candy slipped from his fingers, a bag at a time. He reached the crib on his knees.

He could barely see through his tears. He clutched the rails and pressed his face between two of them, crying so loudly the neighbors could hear him.

Lydia could hear him. He had to shut up.

"Josh." She was at his back, dropping to her knees with her arms around him.

He yanked her close, and for once, she didn't pull away. Choking into her hair, he fought for control.

"We can't do this," she said. "I've been hiding from everything that mattered to me here, and I can't stand seeing you like this. Let's go."

Telling himself to be a man, Josh climbed to his feet and helped Lydia up. Pressing his arm to his eyes, he leaned down for the bags he'd dropped and then followed Lydia.

"I won't go to my parents'," he said. "Forget it."

Stopping in the hall, she nodded. She closed the door, and he swore the pressure on his chest eased.

"I'm going," Lydia said, robbing him of the ability to breathe at all. "You can come. I want you to come, but I'm going."

CHAPTER THREE

"WHAT MAKES my mother and father our answer?" Josh pulled Lydia to face him as she tried to walk away. From such a large man, his insistence should have been intimidating, but she shared his grief and understood his reluctance.

"They're family. We need them, whether you know it or not. I don't care about the past anymore. I want a future."

"With me?"

His taunting barely touched her. "You don't seem to believe me, but yes. Are you coming?"

"Clara's all over that place."

And maybe he was, too—a bereft teenage version of Josh that wouldn't loosen his grip on the grown man. "It might be time to face her and yourself."

"You're a psychologist all of a sudden?"

She shrugged. "Is this house any easier to be in?"

His face turned ruddy, as if he were ashamed of the tears that had turned her back into a fighter. "I haven't stayed in that house for longer than a weekend since I left for college." And he'd left the second he was able to.

She stood, still and silent. He had to decide. She'd made her decision, but she couldn't force Josh to try again.

He turned. She let him reach the stairs before she spoke, and she spoke over the feeling she was strangling.

"Wait."

He stopped without looking back. "What?"

"Maybe I'm not being fair, but I do wish you'd come."

With his back to her, he tensed his shoulders. More eloquent than words, resentment carried him downstairs.

Lydia grabbed at the wall. Suddenly exhausted, she limped to their bedroom. They'd already perfected the silent sharing of a bed, each clinging to one side. She kicked off her shoes, lay down and pulled the quilt Evelyn had given her on her last birthday up to her shoulders.

SITTING AT the family room desk, Josh tried to concentrate on paying the bills that had piled up while Lydia was in the hospital. He ruined four checks and five envelopes.

Memories, never far from his mind, rushed at him, claws outstretched. His parents had been unconscious when he'd come home from his first day of high school. Revolted at the sight of his mother and father sprawled on matching sofas, he'd expected the worst—with no idea how bad it would be. He'd searched the house for Clara.

He'd found her dollhouse, abandoned, her lunch, half eaten. He'd found her body, floating in the filthy swimming pool in their back yard. He couldn't save her. He barely remembered the paramedics dragging him away from Clara after his mother had finally awakened to his screams and dialed 911.

Though he couldn't stop loving his parents, he'd also hated them since that day. Nothing—not a visit, not brainwashing—could change the facts.

But his hard feelings couldn't help Lydia. If she needed comfort—and for some ungodly reason, his parents were love enough for her, how could he refuse to go?

Swearing inside his head, he climbed the stairs. He'd expected to find Lydia reading. Instead, she was burrowed inside a quilt his mom had made for her. The vulnerability of her slight body sealed his fate.

He eased the door shut and started packing the

car. He turned their Halloween candy over to the neighbors, asking them to hand it out, and he packed his clothes. Then, he called his parents.

His father answered. "Josh, is something wrong?"

"Lydia's fine. She mentioned that Mom asked us to come up for a few weeks?"

"Yeah." His dad sounded stunned. Too stunned to make it easier on Josh.

"Well, do you mind if we take her up on that?"

"No, son. Come. Yes, Evelyn, he wants to come up."

His mother's voice came through the phone. "You're coming? I'm so happy. When?"

"Lydia's been napping. I'm going to wake her up so I can pack some of her things. We should be there by dinner."

"Tonight?" He might have offered her the recipe for turning lead into gold. "We'll be ready. I need to make the bed in your old room. We'll have lobster. Bart, run down to the market and get some corn. Even if it's not fresh, it's Lydia's favorite. I think I'll make homemade peach ice cream."

"Okay, Mom. Thanks. I'll call when we're almost there."

"Don't bother. Just come and we'll see you when you get here. Josh, I'm so pleased."

"Thanks for the invite." His parents were already talking to each other when he hung up. He put his bag in the back of the car and spread a sheet on the backseat, hoping he could persuade Lydia to rest on the drive up, rather than sitting for four hours.

Finally, he eased to her side of the bed and rubbed her shoulder. She opened her eyes and focused on him. "Hi."

"Want to go to my mom and dad's?"

She sat up, a hint of light in her eyes at last. "Are you coming?"

As if she'd given him a choice, but he was doing this because she needed it, and he wasn't about to let himself resent her. "Yes."

"When do you want to leave?"

"We just have to pack your things. Tell me what you want and I'll put everything in a bag for you."

"What about Halloween?" She rubbed her face. "I feel as if I'm still asleep."

"I asked Mrs. Dover to hand out our candy." A retired teacher, she had a way with children.

"Good." Lydia grinned. "I'd hate to find our door soaped when we get back."

Hell, he was just relieved she could think of returning. "What do you need?"

She shoved the quilt down to her knees and

crawled out, grimacing as the movement hurt her. "I'll pack for myself."

He got out of her way and dragged her bag from the back of the closet to the end of the bed.

"We should call your mom," she said, grabbing her things.

"I did."

Lydia stood over her suitcase, clothing spilling over her arms. "Evelyn must have fainted."

"She was happy." He'd dreamed of a real family until he was sixteen and they'd come home and brought him back to Kline, Maine, with them. He'd been grateful to escape the foster home where he'd milked cows and felt bitter for nearly two years, but he hadn't expected family life back in Kline. He'd never been able to believe in it or his parents.

"What changed your mind, Josh?"

Still mired in the past, he didn't understand.

She read the question in his eyes. "About going to Maine."

"You needed to see Mom and Dad."

Puzzled, she dropped her clothes and then tried to bunch them into a tidy pile. With a few deft moves, she folded all the pieces that had seeped over the edge of the suitcase. "Thanks."

"Sure."

Before either of them could ruin the moment, he fished out their coats and carried them to the car. When he realized she might try carrying her suitcase down the stairs, he hurtled back inside.

Lydia was putting on his favorite sweater. Soft, green, touchable, a shade that deepened her eyes so that he could barely make himself look away from them. Her head popped out of the V-neck. She looked embarrassed to be caught dressing— by her own husband—and confused about his abrupt return.

"What's up?"

He shook his head, swallowing an accusation that she was treating him like a stranger. "You ready?"

"As soon as I add toiletries." She tossed toothpaste and various other items into her bag, then she brushed her hair into place with her fingers and grabbed her purse off the dresser. "Ready."

He scooped the quilt off the bed. Downstairs, he turned off the lights and then outside, he opened the back passenger door. Lydia hung back. "What?"

He held up the quilt. "I thought you could rest. It's a long drive."

"I'll climb in the back if I get tired."

"Come on, Lydia. Let me have my way. You've been a little more active each day, which I assume means the rest is helping you." Physically, at least.

He couldn't say the silence in their house spelled recovery for either of them.

"I'm all right." She touched his arm, willingly. His chest tightened. "I'm better."

He opened the front door and helped her inside. As soon as he started the engine, she punched in her favorite radio station. Some guy sang about memories of love. Josh glanced at Lydia. Her smile startled him because it came from inside.

He smiled, too, but he had to look away from her. Making her happy felt too good.

THE NEEDLE on the gas gauge was dropping toward a quarter tank as he took the exit for Kline, Maine— named for Reverend Levi Kline, a sixteenth-century hellfire-and-brimstone minister whose influence still obscured most kindness in Josh's hometown.

He drove down a long ramp between tall pines and far-off hardwoods, almost bare of fall leaves. He always felt more like a stranger than a prodigal son. No one in town had mentioned his parents' way with a bottle, but disapproval had followed him down every street.

He'd escaped Kline's small-town, fish-eye interest the morning after he'd graduated from high school. People described New Englanders as stand-offish. Not if you'd grown up among them in a family that provoked notice for all the wrong reasons.

He'd buried himself on the large city campus of Boston College and continued to remain unnoticed through law school. One thing a lobsterman's son could count on in those days of dwindling catches had been plenty of financial aid.

During law school, a Commonwealth Supreme Court judge had selected him as his clerk. Afterward, he'd turned down six-figure starting salaries to keep his unspoken promises. Success often made him forget he was the town drunks' son who wasn't supposed to amount to anything.

Lydia beamed with appreciation at the quaint bandstand on the square and the Victorian houses that lined the west side. "Think of the history the people who've lived in those homes have seen. A woman from Colorado can't even believe places like this are real."

Her excitement annoyed him—like always. "I've got plenty of history—and it's real enough."

"Didn't you know good times here, too?"

"You want the truth? I'm good at my job. People come to me for advice. I get offers—big offers that would mean a lot more to us than a town house." He felt her gaze on him. Her hard gaze. "What?"

"I don't care about offers. I'm beginning to hate

your job. What about us? You can't measure success by our marriage."

"Maybe I don't write you sonnets everyday, but I thought we were safe and settled."

"That makes a girl's heart beat faster." She'd learned a thing or two about sarcasm. "We began growing apart the day you decided I could wait for your free time. Marriage takes effort, too."

Starting to feel harried, he slapped the turn signal to indicate a right.

"Go ahead," she said. "You were saying you're successful."

"Some people think so. I did." Like her, he dropped the argument neither of them was going to win. "But every time I drive down these streets, I'm eighteen again, trying to escape. Look how my parents' neighbors still stare." He nodded at an elderly woman who was already too busy storing up gossip to recognize bitterness in his smile he shot her way. "I hid my family secrets. I let my mother and father make Clara's life a living hell because I had this gut feeling no one else was ever supposed to know what went on behind our doors."

"But didn't you have good times?" Apparently, she had to insist. She pointed ahead of them. "Look at that Founder's Day banner. That means a fair."

"That happened over a month ago."

"Don't they celebrate with a fair? With games and cotton candy?"

"And food for the ducks," he said, remembering the feel of his sister's hand in his. A memory too poignant to face for long. "See that pond on the library side of the square?"

Lydia nodded.

"There's a little cove where those tall reeds grow that has just enough room for two kids. Clara always said it was our spot for feeding the ducks—and they'd swim over the second we started down the hill toward them. I used to take bread for them when I came home."

"Not since I've known you."

"I couldn't without explaining." The truth fought to stay hidden still. "The bad stuff is hard enough to talk about. The good times…" A grown man didn't talk about his breaking heart.

He almost missed the turn by the brick schoolhouse where he and Clara had attended kindergarten. He never passed the ancient church where they'd buried her without anguish that was like a band across his chest.

"We should bring flowers," Lydia said.

Small, square and brown, climbing with ivy, but nowhere near as impressive as the brick edifice erected by new money in the "good" part of Kline, the church felt like ground where Clara would always be waiting. She hadn't been old enough to understand death. Neither had he, but he'd learned in one swift, hard lesson.

Clearing his throat, he turned toward the coast road. "Maybe."

The ocean's salty scent greeted them. His father's family had been lobstermen since—who knew when? Ironically, since Josh and Clara had lived in such poverty, Bart Quincy owned a plot of the richest land in Kline.

Back in the old days, overgrown sea grass had separated the white house from the narrow road. The oversized Cape Cod had looked a little drunk itself, a square, peaked box, in peeling paint gone gray with neglect.

Now a clean picket fence separated Quincy land from folks hiking toward the ocean. Fir trees, holly bushes and a neat lawn bordered the driveway.

"If only you and Clara had known a decent home, maybe you wouldn't be so wedged in the past."

He'd never worried much about himself. It kind of warmed him that Lydia did. "And yet, you don't get that it was my parents' fault?"

"They aren't the same people now."

Always the same answer—and true, but never

good enough. They were headed to what amounted to a homecoming for Lydia and his parents. He'd already started holding his tongue.

He looked at his wife's delicate profile, her large eyes, fringed by long lashes that could feel so soft against his skin, her nose a little large. He'd almost lost her. If coming here comforted her, he'd try to make the best of it and of his parents, too.

Josh opened his fingers on the steering wheel and then tightened them again to follow a slight curve. Usually too aware of consequences to act on impulse, he'd given in to his need to make Lydia happy. Coming home might have been an unforgiving mistake. He'd be stunned if he ended this so-called visit on speaking terms with his wife or his mother and father.

As he parked in a square of loose gravel, his mom slid through the mudroom door beside the kitchen.

He forced himself to smile. Surprise tilted her mouth. She waved. "Even I can tell she's really glad to see me," he said.

"What'd you think?" Lydia sounded mystified. As if love made everything right. Wouldn't their marriage have been as shiny and new-feeling as the day they'd taken their vows if love was all it took? "Is your father home, too?"

"I don't see the truck, but he might have parked in the barn." His parents had converted it to a garage after the last of his grandfather's cows had passed to their bovine reward. "Stay there. I'll help you out."

"Normally, I'd argue, but I feel a little dizzy."

He climbed out and opened her door, searching her face. "Is that normal? Should we call that nurse?"

"I'm just tired." Lydia wrapped her arm around his waist. "The drive felt longer than I expected."

"I can carry you."

She blushed, watching his mother. "No, you can't, but if you don't mind we'll go slowly."

"You made it," Evelyn said. "I was starting to worry."

Josh stared at his mother and at the house. To the right, the ground dipped, just barely, where they'd filled in the pool.

Lydia glanced at him. "Are we late, Evelyn?"

"I was impatient. I'll get the door." She opened it while they climbed the wooden steps. "You look dreadful, Lydia. I'm glad to have you, but I hope the trip wasn't too strenuous."

"I couldn't wait." Lydia hugged his mom. "Where's Bart?"

"Right here." He came around the old pine cupboard and hugged her tight. His smile over her shoulder reached Josh. "I was building a fire in the family room."

"Lydia's headed straight to bed," Evelyn said in a take-no-prisoners tone. "We won't be ready to eat for a while. You have time for a nap." Evelyn tapped her husband's chest. "Get the bags while Josh takes Lydia up."

"Sounds good."

"Thanks for having us," Lydia said. "Josh will come right back to help you, Bart." She tugged his arm. "You should thank them, too."

"Thanks," he mumbled. Josh guided Lydia through the dining room into the small hall that separated the unused "company" living room and the family room from the rest of the house.

"It's too late for you to mediate," Josh said. "Have you noticed how small this place is?"

"I should have considered you'd feel like the walls were trying to squeeze you."

"Don't worry." They started up the staircase. "Whatever happens between my parents and me will come in its own time. I didn't do this for them."

"You don't know you're allowed to love them and be loyal to Clara's memory, too."

"It's not that easy."

"If I could have my mother and father back for even a minute, I'd find the right words to tell them what they mean to me. Think of what you'd say to Clara."

I'm sorry. I'm sorry.

"If you're not careful, you could find too late that you do still care for Evelyn and Bart." No wonder she ate up his parents' uncontrollable need to smother her with love. She stopped, so suddenly she seemed to rock. "The stairs are moving."

"I'm right behind you." Her hair brushed his chin. He wanted to bury his face in the pale strands and tell her to shut up about his mother and father. "Our family, Lydia—the one you and I will have—that matters to me most."

She swallowed. Sick or nervous? He couldn't be sure, but she battled on. "Evelyn and Bart are part of me because I can count on them."

"Can't you understand I tried to believe in them again and again? I gave up when Clara died." At the landing, he moved around her to open his old bedroom door. "Why is this so important to you?"

"Wait." She held on to the newel post. "I never thought of those times—when you believed in them and they let you down. You were just a child." Her troubled gaze looked into his past.

"Stop, Lydia. I don't want you picturing me as a helpless little boy. I don't need pity."

"I've been thinking… You turned your back on

me because you learned how to hold a grudge against your parents. You know how to withhold love."

"It's completely different. They let my sister die—and she depended on me."

"I let your son die—and I was his only protection."

"How can you say that?"

She didn't answer with words. Her eyes were red and full of tears.

"Don't be crazy." He pulled her close. She stiffened, but he held on. "I'm the one who should have seen what was happening. I'm as blind as my parents ever were. Twice now, someone I've loved has died because I wasn't careful enough."

"No." She put her hands on his upper arms, but this time, when she pushed herself away, it was so she could look him in the eye. "You did everything for Clara, and I may be angry because Vivian Durance was your client's wife, but you couldn't know what she'd do unless she told you." She looked at him with a plea for reassurance.

"Of course she didn't tell me. She ranted and the bailiffs dragged her out of court. She didn't even threaten me, much less you. I swear I didn't know."

"You don't have to swear." She braced her hands in the small of her back, sagging against the doorjamb. "I'm exhausted."

She'd let him off the hook, but if they let it go, were they following the same habit that had nearly sunk their marriage? "Come on. A few more steps and you're in bed."

Usually, he had to force himself inside this room. Not this afternoon.

Over the years, he'd taken down most of the old posters. No more scantily clad women seducing from the walls. No cars he'd never own on a public defender's salary. He'd had a thing for Dali when he was a teenager who'd believed human beings could create their own reality. Those posters remained, still in their cheap frames.

"Your mom changed the bedding."

Gone was the thin spread that had barely covered his grandparents' old double bed. His mother had replaced it with an ivory comforter, posh and inviting enough to make Lydia test its thickness.

"Want to change clothes?" he asked.

"Yes, please. These jeans are killing me."

As if on cue, his father showed up, holding their bags. Josh took them. "Thanks, Dad." He set Lydia's on the bed and unzipped the clothing compartment. "What can I take out?"

"I'll get it in a sec." She grinned at his dad. "Thanks, Bart. How's the fishing?"

"Good enough." He hugged her again. Josh

watched, bemused. That sort of spontaneity rarely happened here. "I'm pleased you came, and you know Evelyn and I are both so sorry about the baby."

Lydia faltered. "Me, too, Bart. I've been so swallowed in grief I almost forgot he was your grandson, too." She turned, hiding her face. "Excuse me." She whipped the flap open on her bag and yanked out a pair of flannel pajama pants and a matching blue tank top. Without looking back, she left to change in the bathroom across the hall.

Josh stared at his father. Over Bart's shoulder, Clara's room was closed tight, decades of accusations and grief stuffed inside.

"I'm glad you found time to come, son."

"I want to be with Lydia." His father flinched and Josh looked away from Clara's room. "We're grateful you and Mom offered her—us— time up here."

"Come down when you're ready." Bart started to leave but looked back. "Concentrate on Lydia. Don't either of you worry about us this visit."

Josh exhaled, seeing stars in front of his eyes. Maybe Lydia was right. He had to do something about this thing with his parents.

He moved his bag to the chair at his childhood desk, which was rammed against the wall beneath the sloping eave. He was hanging Lydia's things in the closet when she came back. "Where's your father?"

"Downstairs." Josh pulled back the comforter and sheet. "In you go." As she crawled past him, he stroked her back. She jumped, but kept moving, unconsciously choosing her usual side of the bed.

"What did you say to him?"

"You don't have to be suspicious. We didn't argue."

"Nice effort." She eased onto her back. "Wake me if your parents want to put dinner off because I'm sleeping." She rolled on to her side and pulled the sheet up.

"They won't mind if you sleep." He tucked the comforter around her. No task was too small.

"They're doing enough, getting us out of that house. I don't want to put them to extra trouble." She sighed, so weary her skin and lips looked almost bloodless. "Is this worse for you?" she asked.

"No." Seeing the baby's things had made him hurt for Lydia and himself and for the child they'd never have a chance to know. He'd never feel comfortable in Kline, but time had applied a sturdy bandage to the wounds he'd suffered there. "Being here is better than being in the town house."

CHAPTER FOUR

EVELYN WAS CHOPPING tomatoes for a salad when a scream rode up her spine. She dropped the knife. Her hand, jerking, shoved the tomatoes across the counter. She flew down the hall and up the narrow stairs.

At the door to Josh's room, she paused. Lydia might want privacy. Hell, no. She'd screamed. No one would ever find Evelyn negligent again.

"Lydia?" Tapping twice, she opened the door at the same time. "Are you awake, honey?"

"Come in."

Already in, Evelyn stopped dead. Covered in sweat that curled her blond hair, Lydia turned from the closet beside Josh's desk, her hand sliding off the doorknob to tremble at her thigh. Her pale face and shadowed eyes made Evelyn desperate to do something. Anything.

"How bad do I look?" Lydia asked.

"Well." Evelyn didn't want to frighten her.

"I hope you're feeling some better. What's wrong?"

"Nothing. I thought I'd lost my clothes." She opened the closet and pulled out a clean T-shirt, her face flushing as if she'd made up an excuse. "Josh must have put them away."

"You didn't scream over a shirt."

Lydia froze. "I screamed? You heard me?"

"Yes." Trying to laugh, Evelyn pushed Lydia's moist hair away from her face. "That's the way screaming works. Do you have a fever?"

"Don't suggest that in front of Josh." Lydia's quick smile apologized for her terseness. "He'll worry."

Evelyn sank against the bed, pushing her hands down her own faded jeans. "What a relief. Bart and I wondered if something was wrong between you."

Lydia stared too hard at her shirt. "We're both sad."

"I mean I've been worried before. Josh has a compulsion to save the world. It's my fault, of course, and his father's, so I shouldn't say anything, but where does that leave you?"

Lydia shook out her shirt, her expression an order to butt out. "I need to change."

The old Evelyn would have backed down. The

new Evelyn wasn't so different after all. "Go in the bathroom and wash your face, too. I'll make the bed. You're sure about the fever?"

Lydia started toward the door, but stopped. "Look," she said. "Josh hasn't done anything. I fell asleep, and every time I fall asleep, I dream I haven't lost the baby. Then comes a moment when I know I have."

The lump in Evelyn's throat refused to go down. "None of this is your fault, and Josh won't hate you for it." She grabbed the comforter and fluffed it hard enough to almost remove the batting.

Lydia tossed her shirt on the bed and pulled Evelyn close. "Josh doesn't know what to do with his feelings and neither do I. I'm starting to think it's an everyday, take-stock-of-where-you-stand process." Her hand was tender on the top of Evelyn's head.

"Josh loves you. Don't forget that."

"He loves you, too, but he lets his relationships slide, and I kept waiting around for our marriage to get better. I'm not content to coast anymore."

"You and I are in the same place, and Josh is about to find himself at a disadvantage." Evelyn piled the comforter on the desk chair. "I wanted you here because I love you and I needed to take care of you, but I have an ulterior motive. I've missed my son. I'm going to find a way to make him believe in us again."

Lydia looked askance, which gave Evelyn her first doubt. "What?"

"I'm not sure Josh is easy to force."

"He's here."

"Because we were both desperate to get away."

"Then you'll remain desperate. I'm not above scheming to get my son back in my life."

"What does Bart think?" Lydia asked it with pity in her voice, as if she were hoping Bart could make Evelyn come to her senses. Dread tried to rush in, but Evelyn turned it back.

"Don't worry. We'll be fine. Now, I'll make this bed. You freshen up and come sit with me if you feel able while I start supper."

They sidestepped each other. Evelyn raced around the bed plumping and straightening. Fear of losing a son would light a fire under any woman.

Lydia shut the bathroom door, and a moment later, the water began to run. Evelyn finished the bed and then turned to Josh's open bag. Jeans and sweaters, neatly stacked, just begged to be put away.

Except that her son would consider her intrusive if she took care of his personal things. She set the bag on a shelf halfway down the closet wall and closed the door. Then she tidied the room, ending by picking up a copy of *Tom Sawyer* from the desk. Bart's father had given him that book. She pressed it to her face, taking solace in the musty smell of the rough, old-fashioned cloth binding.

"Where's Josh?"

Evelyn jumped, but then quickly stashed the book on the shelf above the desk. "He had phone calls. Last I saw him, he was strolling the headland with his cell phone glued to his ear."

"Working. What a bolt from the blue." Lydia grasped the door to hold herself up.

"Are you all right?" As concerned about Lydia's indignation as her lack of balance, Evelyn took her arm. "Let me help you down the stairs."

"I'm fine. Really—and I shouldn't have said anything."

They headed downstairs. Over the front door, a small fanlight let in sunshine, mottled by hundred-year-old glass. How many times had she felt as if she was searching for her own future when she'd tried to see through that glass?

Evelyn couldn't bear to look at Lydia. "He's not out there making appointments in the city." She finally realized her son had always taken another tack to solve his problems. Business had come before family but not anymore. "I'd bet he's canceling everything that would take him back to that office. He'll be here until you're ready to go back."

"That could be forever, Evelyn."

"CANCEL THAT CONFERENCE, Brenda, and make sure we get continuances on the rest of my cases." Josh cupped his hand over his free ear as late autumn wind kicked through the sea grass, rustling it in loud whispers. A storm was coming in on clouds that seemed to have blown up in the blue-gray sky.

"Cancel everything? For the next three weeks?"

His assistant's shock hardly flattered him under the circumstances. Where else did she think he'd be than with his wife? "I'll let you know if anything changes, but don't expect to hear from me."

"You have no idea when you'll be back?" she said again.

"Right. Talk to Dean." The chief public defender "I told him I'd be here until Lydia is well. He knows you're going to bring him my caseload. He may want to reassign my cases."

"You're not quitting, Josh?"

"No." Below the cliff, high tide slammed into the dirt and rock walls. He couldn't give up, not even for Lydia.

Brenda tapped at her keyboard. "I'll follow your instructions, but you'll let me know if you decide you're not coming back?"

"Yeah."

"Because I want to choose my own boss."

So he'd be missed? He shook his head. She was good enough that the other attorneys would line up to interview her. "Thanks, Brenda." He hung up and turned toward the house.

He was standing on his own land. Side by side with his parents' lot, it was too close to them, but—he turned out to sea, where the sky had grown even darker and the clouds dipped into the water—his headland was beautiful.

He stopped for his fill of the view he'd never see through his own windows. In the sweep of the wind, he searched for a sense of family ties that should bind him here. His grandfather had left a parcel for him and a parcel for Clara. After his sister's death, her land had been merged with his father's property.

Lydia used to ask him if he'd ever be able to live here one day. He knew she'd move tomorrow. She'd probably already planned their house in her head. She'd never throw those ideas away now.

She'd told him once that she looked at the headland as their escape from Hartford. She wanted to be close to the reformed Evelyn and Bart Quincy.

He'd been two years from adulthood when the state had returned him to their newly sober care. They'd sat him down and blah-blah-blahed about starting over.

But he'd known that song by heart. He'd spent eighteen months mourning for his sister and for his pathetic boyhood dream of finding a happy, safe home for them both.

He'd been Clara's only semblance of a parent. The first time he'd tried to make her dinner, he'd found a vodka bottle in the potato bin. Why did they make the labels so pretty to a boy? He'd unscrewed the lid, sniffed and nearly thrown up. He'd found another in the storage bench in the mudroom when he was hunting for Clara's boots so he could walk her to preschool. His first day working the lobster boat, he'd discovered another bottle in his father's toolbox.

He wiped his face. Images so frightening to a child enraged him as a man. And Lydia liked being with those monsters.

He put on some speed, knowing logically that they wouldn't—couldn't—hurt Lydia, but every time he saw how much she loved them, his past pain came up and slapped him in the face.

The mudroom door slammed against the side of the house. Lydia came out. At first she looked as if she was running away. Then he realized the high wind had snatched the door out of her hand. She leaned back in to turn on the porch light and then pushed the door shut with both hands.

He jogged to her. "Are you all right?"

"Fine." She searched him—for the phone he'd slipped into his pocket, probably. "Your mother said you had to call the office?"

"I gave Brenda the lowdown on my cases." Relief smoothed Lydia's frown. "You and I have a long way to go."

"Before we trust each other?" The wind swooped at her hair.

He climbed the stairs toward her and stopped when she was only inches away. "I trust you." He was trying, anyway. "I put my cases in Brice Dean's hands."

"Thanks," she said, and he was grateful for her simple reply. "What if he fires you?"

"He might," Josh said. Without conceit, he added, "but I'm good."

"I don't want Brice Dean to make that decision for us."

"Now that I've left Hartford for a couple of weeks, you want me to quit my job?" Let it go, let it go. He knew Lydia better than that. She'd never try to manipulate him.

"I won't pretend I can imagine wanting to go back." She'd borrowed one of his dad's jackets from the mudroom. He bunched the lapels.

"I know." They were both too upset to make long-term demands or decisions. "Let's go in, out of the cold and dark."

"Your mom's about to murder the lobster."

His now toughened wife couldn't take the "senseless slaughter." Trying not to grin, he brushed the back of his hand over her cheekbone. So soft, her skin. "You'll eat?" The urge to kiss her was strong. She could still want him. He knew it, but his capacity for rejection was wearing thin. "You need to gain back the weight you've lost."

She squeezed his fingers briefly, but Josh and Lydia had lost their ability to offer mutual comfort. "I'm a hypocrite. I feel bad for those poor lobsters, but I plan to eat my share and clean up everyone else's plates."

"My father's always admired your appetite." Josh was relieved she felt up to eating.

"He's in for an impressive show."

LYDIA HAD OVERESTIMATED her abilities. To celebrate their homecoming, his mother had set the table in the dining room. Bathed in candlelight that lent her healthy color, Lydia took the chair across from Josh's and dug in. She made a respectable job of the tail and the smaller claw, but lost interest in the pincer.

"Something wrong?" His dad disapproved of her surrender. "You haven't touched your corn."

"After you shucked it yourself, Lydia," Evelyn said.

"I wondered why we were eating strings tonight." Josh made a show of removing a corn silk from his teeth.

"Save it and you can use it for floss later," his mother said. "Waste not, want not."

Josh laughed, surprising himself as much as his parents. Lydia seemed to fade as she laughed, too. "You're tired," he said.

She glanced from him to his mother and then to his father. "I'm fine." In other words, *don't turn me into an invalid.*

"I know you don't like to give in." He set down his own fork. "But until you're well, you lie down whenever you're tired." He slid his napkin onto the table as his mother stood. "Mother, leave the dishes. I'll do them later."

"Huh?" They all three said it together.

He'd hardly suggested carrying his grandmother's best china down to the cliff and tossing it over. "You've worked all afternoon to make us comfortable. Let me clean the kitchen."

He helped Lydia scoot out her chair. She glanced up at him and then smiled at her mother-in-law. "Do what he says, Evelyn."

"If you say so…."

Josh helped Lydia back to their room, puzzled by her silent submission. "How bad do you feel?"

"I'm sore," she said with a heavy sigh, "and exhausted. It'll pass."

Was it normal? He waited, feeling both foolish and uneasy beside the bathroom door while she brushed her teeth. After her third self-conscious glance, he turned away. Maybe women didn't like their husbands to stare at them while they foamed with toothpaste. She stepped out when she was finished.

"Need some help?" he asked.

"No." She was drying her hands on a soft yellow towel. "When you go back downstairs, you'll be nice?"

"Nice?" She'd never understand. "When am I not nice?"

"I mean really—not that fake stuff you all do." She glanced down the stairs. "All of you."

"What's on your mind now?"

"I talked with your mother this afternoon." She tried to smooth out his frown with her fingertips.

He dragged her palm to his mouth. God, she smelled good. Her touch eased his pain. As if the tide of his need pushed her away, she eased her hand out of his and climbed into bed—clearly not welcoming company.

"What's my mother up to?"

Lydia shook her head, her posture a flawless picture of guilt. "She has to be up to something?"

"I'm glad lying isn't your talent."

"I felt guilty not telling you—"

"We're here because you—and I—couldn't stay at home. Whatever my mom's plotting won't work. 'Night, Lydia."

"You're sure?"

"I don't care about games. It's always the same thing, trying to drag me back here." He took advantage of her relief, leaning across the bed to kiss her forehead. Every time she let him this close, he remembered he'd almost lost her, too. For those first few hours in the hospital, no one could or would tell him she was going to live. Fighting a compulsion to wrap her in his arms, he backed off the bed and headed toward the hall.

"Josh, I've sometimes thought of you as a hard man—but maybe you're not."

She was half asleep so he didn't answer, but her words would stay with him. He eased the door shut and went downstairs. His mother had already cleaned the kitchen.

"Would you like some coffee?" she asked, gesturing to the cup in front of his father at the kitchen table.

"No, thanks." He glanced at the real estate ads in the newspaper his father was reading. "What are you doing, Dad?"

"I never get to read the paper in the morning before I go out on the boat. Want a section?"

Surely his mother wasn't looking for a home for him and Lydia. She'd lost more than her lack of subtlety. How could she even think he'd move back here?

"I'm going for a walk," he said. As he took his coat off the hook in the mudroom, he remembered it was Halloween. "Don't you get any children out this way?" There'd been few when he was a child.

"I have some candy." His mother nodded toward a bowl on the counter. "But we'll probably be eating it for the next year."

"Too few neighbors." Josh's dad peered over his reading glasses. "The kids go for quantity since those new subdivisions went in on the other side of town."

"A lot of young families live out there. They even voted in a bond to build a new elementary school."

Josh was smiling as he put on his coat. Outside, he walked around the house, glad Lydia had wanted to tell him about his mother's plans, even if there'd been no need.

He hunched into his collar. His coat was no match for an unseasonably cold night. Storms had flirted with the coast all day long, and the clouds still spiraled in front of the moon. He went down the cliff, all the way to his parents' closest neighbor, a retired politician from some Midwestern state, who'd fallen in love with Maine during his eastern tenure in congress. Josh knew the name, but he'd never met the man.

They'd torn down a Cape Cod that had looked like his own family's. In its place, they'd built a house in layers of limestone and windows. Lydia, who'd spent her career restoring historical buildings and homes would disparage the modern lines, but Josh was drawn to the orange-colored lamplight within, a seductive sense of welcoming heat built into the cliff.

A man walked past one of four wide-paned windows, and Josh turned away, feeling a bit as he had as a boy, like a peeping Tom who couldn't resist looking inside other people's houses to find out what a real family did together.

As he went back home, fighting a wind that seemed to be needle-tipped in ice, he saw the porch light at the front door. Otherwise, the house was dark. He turned the doorknob, half expecting it to be locked, but they'd remembered he was out there.

He eased up the stairs, smiling wryly. He wasn't a child anymore; his parents could at least be counted on to offer him a bed and not expect him to sleep outside if he didn't show up before their early bedtime.

He washed up and stripped down to boxers and a T-shirt and felt his way across his childhood bedroom in the dark. Lydia lay on her side, her back to him. The moonlight caught strands of her hair. He reached out to touch her, but stopped, uncertain of his welcome, positive she needed sleep.

He willed his mind to shut off. Pictures formed in front of his eyes—that empty crib, the cold headland. His mother, looking so hopeful, his father gruff. A horrifying memory of Clara in that hellish green water.

He turned, his heart pounding so hard he felt dizzy. Suddenly, Lydia rolled over and sneaked one hand into the space between them. She massaged his side.

He covered her hand, breathing hard. Could she know how much she meant to him? He needed to matter to her.

After a few minutes, she moved back onto her side. Her soft groan broke his heart as she dragged the blanket over her.

Josh flattened his palm against his T-shirt where she'd touched him. They weren't through talking about her terms for staying. She hated his job, and she was going to force the issue. They both knew it was coming. She might have been saying goodbye or she might have been comforting him.

He chose to hope she'd decided to stay.

CHAPTER FIVE

JOSH WOKE FIRST the next morning. The air outside was fresh and the sky blue. The mudroom door, below his room, slammed. He knew, having seen many blue mornings in the past, that his father was leaving to work on the boat.

Hard work and forgetfulness. He could use some of that.

Struggling out of the sheets, he went to the window. Cold snaked around his body.

"You want to go with him?"

He turned back. With a sleepy smile, Lydia curved one arm above her head.

"Did I wake you?" he asked.

"I've been enjoying the warmth. This place gets chilly at night."

"Dad turns off the heat." He laughed at a memory not wrapped in resentment. "He never got over the energy shortages in the seventies."

"Better call him before he gets to the garage."

He slid his fingers into the two notches at the bottom of the window frame and tugged. His mother had washed the cowboy curtains till they were practically see-through, and someone had done a fair job of refurbishing layer after layer of the same old paint. He finally jerked it open. "Dad?"

His father turned from the barn door.

"Wait while I dress. I'll come with you."

His dad froze with underwhelming enthusiasm. "Thanks, but maybe Lydia needs you."

"Not that much," Lydia said from the bed.

Josh glanced back. "Nice."

She lifted both arms and stared him down with a dry smile, which he returned.

He'd become the sensitive type.

"She says not. I'll get ready and come down."

His father nodded. "Take your time. I have to load some new rope for the boat."

"I don't think he's in on Mom's plan," Josh said to Lydia.

She laughed. "He doesn't like long silent spaces."

"We'll stop at Gordon's for donuts and coffee," his father shouted.

"We're wrong," Lydia said.

Little did she know. Stopping at the donut shop had been Josh's favorite treat. Like all little sisters, Clara had copied her big brother. They'd begged many Sunday mornings for breakfast at Gordon's. When their parents wouldn't go, he and Clara had searched the sofas and chairs for change and walked to the bakery by themselves.

He waved at his father and shut the window. The moment he turned, Lydia dropped her arms. "What?"

"Nothing." He hid his expression in a search for last night's jeans and sweater, but as he reached for the waistband on his boxers, he stopped. Uncomfortable in front of his own wife, he considered crossing the hall to the bathroom. What the hell? Who needed a shower to work on a boat? Shivering, he hurried into his clothes. "You don't mind if I leave you alone?"

"I'm fine. Have a good time."

"Yeah." He leaned down, intending to kiss her, because they'd always kissed goodbye—even at the worst times. Too many brush-offs in the past few days stopped him. He squeezed her shoulder instead. It felt thinner.

"Bye, Josh."

"I'll bring you a fish."

"Cool. What about an aquarium?"

He laughed. "You must be feeling better. I meant to eat." He stopped at the door. "Don't go out unless you're feeling up to it."

"I won't."

Something in her eyes drew him back. Sadness shadowed her gaze, made her seem almost defenseless, but she'd never needed anyone to take care of her.

There was a difference between needing and wanting to be cared for. Maybe she'd just never asked him.

"You're sure you don't mind if I go?" He circled the bed to take her hand.

"I want you to. Have fun." Her mouth curved, and the sadness flickered out. "Work hard for Bart."

"Try to take it easy."

She nodded, and they shared one of those long, silent spaces his father didn't like. He stroked her fingers, and she curled them around his.

"I'm trying to find a medium," he said, "between smothering you and putting you first."

"I'm trying to believe it's not just for now."

"And when we go back home, I'll go back to work and forget you?"

"I'm not sure I can go home."

His mouth went dry. "This isn't 'love me and leave me.' We're talking about our marriage."

"You know I've tried." She rose on her knees, her face flushed. "I'm sorry I brought it up now."

"You're asking me to quit my job and move."

"I guess I am. I want to wake up every morning like we did today, in peace and quiet, with no fear. No horrible crimes waiting for you, no crazy killers lurking where I work."

"Be rational, Lydia." He could have chosen a more sympathetic response.

Her skin grew pinker by the second. "I'm sorry. We can talk when you come back."

"I can't just go." But what would he say if he stayed?

"You can." She pushed her hair back.

"Your timing—"

"I know, but moving away from Hartford has been on my mind for years. You just haven't listened."

"Maybe I didn't want to hear."

"And now, Josh?"

"Now, I think this is too important to decide when my father's waiting."

"Because your life is there?"

He looked around the room that had been half safe harbor and half perdition in his childhood. "I'm trying to tell you in every way I can that my life is with you." He felt so betrayed, "I love you" wouldn't come.

"Okay, okay." Waving him toward the door, she

sat back on her feet, looking mortified. The longer he stayed, the more resentful he grew, so he left.

His wife, embarrassed, and he, furious to hear the demand he'd dreaded. And that was normal for a marriage?

He wasn't a man who held a divining rod to his own emotions, but he knew he didn't want a marriage where his wife shamed herself by speaking her mind. He couldn't find an answer beyond his frustration.

He went to the kitchen in search of coffee. His mother set the brewer on a timer each night, and she left cups and the sugar bowl beside the coffeemaker.

It was later than his father usually left, but he was still surprised to find his mom up to her elbows in cookie dough.

"Josh." For a second she looked like Clara, caught being naughty.

If he didn't want to talk to his wife, he certainly didn't want a cozy chat with his mother.

He reached for a mug.

She grabbed a towel that stuck to her hands. "What are you doing?"

"Going with Dad." Pouring coffee, he eyed the sugary-looking dough, spiked with chocolate chips. "You're up early."

"I'm making cookies."

Her slender body couldn't shield the massive mixing bowl at her back. "For an army?" It kind of pissed him off. For Clara's only school-aged birthday, he'd helped his little sister make a dozen rocklike cupcakes they'd iced with watery cream cheese frosting.

"For no one in particular." His mother slapped the water faucet on and stabbed at the stream of water. She tapped soap from the bottle beside the sink into one palm and then scrubbed until her hands turned red.

Josh took a swig of coffee. "You must have enough for four dozen, Mother."

She composed herself. "Six."

He upturned his coffee mug into the sink. Cookies might have made Clara feel cared for years ago. A whole bakery would be too late, now.

"Six dozen?" He washed his cup. "Why so many?"

With a spoon the size of a small, wooden shovel, she stirred her mixture. "I'm selling them at Gordon's."

"Gordon's?"

"They sell cookies now, too." She crossed to a stack of square papers by the fridge and held up the top sheet. "By Grandma Trudy." Eye-catching orange and yellow surrounded a sprightly grandma-type sporting a huge cornucopia that spilled cookies behind her.

"For Thanksgiving?" He set the label down and then straightened it on the counter. "Why are you doing this?"

"Why not? I started with Halloween-themed cookies. Your dad said I worked a spell on the recipe."

"You're Grandma Trudy." He pointed at the wrappers. "I don't get it."

"I started my own business. In fact, I'm doing so well at Gordon's, Geraldine Dawson's been helping me look for my own building."

"Geraldine Dawson?" She'd been his teacher a million years ago.

"Sure. She's retired, but she finds herself looking after her twin grandsons." Evelyn closed down, a New England woman who'd exposed more town gossip than she meant to. Which meant there was more she hadn't said about the Dawsons. "She needs some extra money so she's gotten her real estate license."

Josh cut to the chase. "Are you and Dad in trouble?" Fishermen still didn't rake in the bucks. His mom had never set foot out of the house for a job except to work his father's boat when they couldn't find another hand.

"I knew you'd be upset. I just don't know why."
She looked at him, her face tight. "Make me understand you. Just this once."

"I'm not upset and you don't have to look guilty." He backed away. "I just never expected you to start a business and I'm surprised. Better go." As he reached the door, she caught him.

"What about you helping me look for a place?"

"What?" This must be "the plan." He tried to free his arm, but his mother held on. "You have Mrs. Dawson."

"I need legal advice, too."

He had the perfect excuse. It wasn't his expertise, but his mother's face was so earnest. "Maybe." Yet, what he meant was—don't involve me. "Lydia and I are only here for a few weeks."

"That's plenty of time."

"Your plan won't work."

"Lydia told you we talked?"

"She didn't go into details, but she's my wife, Mom. We don't keep secrets." Except about their own feelings.

"I want you to be part of your father's and my lives again."

Lydia, in his head, begged him to be kind. He grappled with a smile that hurt. Everyone who mattered to him needed him to change. Right now. Today.

His father honked the truck horn. Salvation. "We'll talk at dinner."

Escaping, he slammed the mudroom door and ran to meet his father, who'd begun to roll down the driveway in his battered, pale blue truck. A classic if it weren't so neglected. Maybe Grandma Trudy'd help his father replace the thirty-year-old pickup, he thought with an unwilling smile.

Josh climbed in, pounding the dashboard with an open hand and fake good humor. "She still runs."

"Yeah," his dad said. "Let's move. The fish won't wait." He started down the driveway. Several miles brought them to the edge of town.

"When did Mom start making these cookies?"

His dad's head turned as if it were on a swivel. "Her business bothers you?"

"I know I'm wrong to resent it, but imagine how much easier 'Grandma Trudy' would have made life for Clara and me."

"You're talking about the past, Josh. Won't you ever be able to let it go?"

He seemed to feel Josh's rush of anger. "I'm not asking you to forget, but to try forgiving."

He wanted to do as his mother and father and wife had all asked, but despite their jack hammering and his best intentions, he still felt the loss of everything his parents' negligence had denied him and Clara.

"What's the big secret?"

"I didn't realize she planned to tell you so soon."

"One of the ironies of my childhood was that my mom was a great cook, but she never bothered."

Bart stared straight ahead, white-knuckling the steering wheel. "Evelyn's a good woman. A clean and sober woman." Bart eyed him with the righteous anger of a father and husband. "And she's your mother."

"Sorry." He tapped the dashboard close to his father's hand. "I meant that. I'm sorry."

His dad turned onto Kline Street and swerved into the closest open spot in front of Gordon's. "I don't want you to feel sorry." He opened the door. "You refuse to give up on strangers. And I'll never give up on you."

Josh stared at the truck's floor, helpless, strangled by the sorrow of his father's loss, too. He'd wanted his boy, had planned baseball games and bike rides and hikes through the park—all the fun he'd have loved to have shared with his dad.

No matter how he rationalized it, his job *was* partly to blame for his own son's death, and the town house, their neighborhood, the city would never look the same to him or to Lydia. "Let's go to work, Dad." He inhaled the salt-laden, cold air. The perfume of his youth. "I need to think."

"YOU'RE MAKING COOKIES for a living? And Josh said he'd help you?" How was that even possible? "Am I still asleep?" Lydia asked.

"He said maybe." Evelyn poured coffee while Lydia held the mug in both hands. "Oh, that one's chipped, honey. Let me get you another."

"No, no." Lydia sipped. "Tell me what you said to Josh."

"I told him the truth. I want us to be closer, and I need his help. He's part of my family, you know. Families help each other." She wiped her hand on a towel printed with beaming lobsters. "Maybe I didn't say all that, but he's a smart man. He deduced what I couldn't say."

"You didn't start this business just to lure Josh home? You must have put money into this already. You could lose all your investment."

"I'm using the business to reach my son, but I'm serious about it, Lydia. I'm small potatoes right now, but this idea is my own." Her pride fueled a bright smile. "All mine, something worthwhile and profitable, good work."

"Why not let Josh see that? You don't have to

involve him to make him see you're sticking to it. Isn't that the point? That you're trustworthy?"

"He'd have to be blind not to realize I stick to my promises and responsibilities now. What he doesn't see is that he still deserves a mother and father, and he's not betraying Clara if he lets himself be our son again."

"How will a cookie business achieve that?" Lydia drank more coffee.

"I need his help as much as anyone does. I'm buying property and sinking our savings into a company. I'll need legal advice." She wiped her hands again. "He can't resist a challenge, and he's incapable of turning down a cry for help."

"He's not an expert on corporate law."

"He'll research." Evelyn began to wrap the cookies with flying fingers. Then she added a colorful sticker marked "Grandma Trudy" to seal each wrapper. "I've tied myself to this house for years, trying to prove I could be a good mother, a decent homemaker."

Evelyn turned "homemaker" into a slur. "I want to be if I have another child." Lydia had never considered leaving her job before now. During her pregnancy she'd planned for day care, but her priorities had changed.

Caught up in her own emotions, Evelyn continued as if Lydia hadn't spoken. "I've been trying to make Josh see I've been a good mother for a lot longer than I was a bad one. I started dying inside these walls again when I realized that nothing I did made Josh see I've changed."

Lydia set her mug down so hard the coffee sloshed. "You mean you wanted a drink? That's why you drank before? Because you didn't like being home? With Josh?"

Frustration emanated from Evelyn's spare body. "You blame us too?" she asked quietly.

"Josh is my first concern." Lydia didn't want to hurt Evelyn, but suddenly she wanted to protect Josh. "I won't ever tell him why you drank. What happened with Clara isn't truly any of my business."

"You're family."

"I won't take sides."

"You can't choose only the good things when you marry into a family." Evelyn slapped a wrapper on the last cookie. "You're caught in the middle."

The words reproached Lydia. "Could you be right?" She wiped the coffee off Evelyn's spotless counter.

The other woman looked up, fear that she'd gone too far in her eyes. "Right? I'm sorry. I've been thinking about my own problems with Josh. I shouldn't have suggested..."

"But am I detached? Can that be true?" Walking away was easier than working to save a dying marriage.

Evelyn caught her hand. "I didn't mean to upset you."

"You're right." She'd acted as though everything was okay at home. Then she'd gone about her own life as if Josh had no say in her decisions. The work she'd accepted, the hours she'd undertaken. She hadn't even asked him to help her search for child care.

Deep down, she'd believed he might not be around to have his say. She'd never think like that again. She couldn't let herself if she was committed to having more children with Josh.

"You're not thinking of leaving him?" Evelyn tugged at the short curls on her forehead. She and Bart had salvaged their marriage out of the worst tragedy. "Tell me I'm wrong."

"You are," Lydia said, punctuating her declaration with a smile. "Don't try to distract me from what you're doing with these cookies." She reached for one, swearing silently at her trembling hand. She sniffed the butter and brown sugar and the indefinable warmth of home cooking. "How long have you been hiding this talent?"

"Lydia, what about my son?"

"You have to let it go."

"I don't. I'm his mother."

"I'm his wife."

Evelyn stared at her with a hint of antagonism. "You must know how much he loves you."

For some reason, Evelyn's certainty threatened to raise Lydia's doubts again. She didn't answer.

Finally, the other woman sighed. "Okay." She took stock of the kitchen as if it were all new to her, including the well-worn cookie sheets stacked in the sink.

She nodded toward the cookie Lydia had reached for before. "Try one. I love to cook, but Bart has high cholesterol, no matter what we eat or how much I make him exercise."

Lydia tried to imagine Bart in his faded jeans, white thermal T-shirt and faded plaid flannel shirt, jogging the neighborhood in the latest running shoes. It was easier to picture him bench pressing the boat.

"Where'd you come up with the name?"

"Trudy was my grandmother." Lydia opened the stove for a quick peek at the next batch. "I use her recipes."

Lydia took a bite. "Mmm—it's delicious," she said, through a melt-in-her-mouthful.

Evelyn opened the fridge.

"Did you forget something?"

"Yeah. Cookies do not a breakfast make." She pulled out the egg carton. "Though you'll never taste better than mine."

Lydia fingered a few crumbs off her upper lip and then licked them off her finger. "What if Josh turns you down, Evelyn?"

Her mother-in-law ignored that suggestion. "Two eggs? Cheddar cheese? Mushrooms?" She leaned into a cupboard beside the sink and plucked out an onion. "You wouldn't ease my mind and let me toss in a hunk of ham or some bacon?"

"Answer me."

Evelyn set her eggs and produce beside a cutting board. "He can't. If he does, I..." She looked up finally, a bit of dough in her springy hair. "I don't know what I'd do."

Lydia stared at her. Around them, the kitchen clock ticked and the oven bell rang. She should have thought about her timing before she'd asked Josh to leave Hartford, but she was just as desperate as Evelyn for his answer. He had to choose her over that job. Their life together had to come first.

She walked to the bread box and took out a loaf. "You want some toast?"

"One slice." Evelyn opened another cupboard and took out the toaster. A glance at Lydia made her pause. "Something's wrong."

Lydia tried to shake her head. She plugged in the toaster and inserted the bread. Evelyn began cutting tomatoes.

"You can talk to me. I've confided my worst secrets in you today." Evelyn's laugh rode on the gravel of long-ago cigarettes and the false hope she'd found in a vodka bottle. She sounded more real than Lydia had ever heard her.

"It's nothing. Just change. You want it. I need it—with all my heart." Hartford stood for disappointment and unspoken dissension and dread that had turned into justified fear. A tear sizzled on the silver toaster.

Evelyn dropped her knife. "I upset you."

Lydia shook her head. "It's the baby." And the fact that Josh could hold a grudge for decades. And her own hopeless longing to escape pain and fear that seemed to smother her in that town house.

"You can fight grief a little, but sometimes you just have to abide until it takes its fingers out of your heart." From behind, Evelyn slid her arms around Lydia's waist. Shaking, Lydia hung on.

She cried for Josh's comfort, too. All the wishing in the world couldn't change anything that had happened, couldn't teach either of them to forgive.

"Hey," Evelyn said, "no more crying. I hate seeing you so sad."

"I swing from hope to grief," Lydia said. "Can't seem to help it."

"It's called healing," Evelyn said against her hair.

CHAPTER SIX

IT WAS ONLY when Lydia had to weave through weekend traffic on the busy square that she realized it was Saturday. Remnants of the previous night's Halloween celebrations—which hadn't reached out to the house on the cliff, blew around the cars and the wrought-iron fences.

In the swift breeze of an oncoming storm that had dotted the sky with clouds, children wandered, weary, at their parents' sides. Moms and dads hauled their sons and daughters by unwilling hands, strangely oblivious, in their rush to finish a weekend's errands.

Lydia parked in front of Lillian Taylor's. *The Florist* wound in vinelike lettering up Lillian's window. As Lydia opened the car door, her phone rang.

It was Evelyn. They'd finished breakfast, shared a walk down the headland and discussed fish chowder for supper. Then she'd showered, read the paper and stared at the news channel on TV.

After lunch, she'd left without telling Evelyn where she was headed. This task was private, something she wanted to do for Josh.

"Hey," she said.

"Where are you? I went up to gather the laundry and when I came back you'd disappeared."

"I'm in town. I yelled up the stairs." She'd raised her voice a little.

"What are you doing? Josh is going to kill me if you make yourself sick."

"I won't, and you're not responsible for me. I'll be back soon, Evelyn. Need anything from the shops?"

"Hmmm. We could use some bread. Something crisp on the outside, nice and soft in the middle."

Lydia's mouth watered. "Sounds good."

She shut her phone and went inside the florist's. She quickly settled on a bouquet of wildflowers and daisies, just right for a little girl. Lillian wrapped the stems in cellophane for her and found a green vase. Afterward, Lydia went down to the bakery and picked up a hot baguette that only made her more hungry. She added a bottle of water to her shopping.

Then she drove to the church and parked

outside the fence that bordered the cemetery. For just a second, sadness reached out with its spindly fingers, but she fought it off.

Clara had been gone a long time. People only remembered her with sadness. Lydia intended to add a little hope to the mix. She didn't want to think of her lost son with only sadness in eighteen years.

She walked around the fence. Many of the headstones sat crooked. Most were tinted green. She strode up and down, pulling off the occasional vine, plucking dead flowers from old urns. At a stone that said, Quincy, Infant, April 1782, she added a couple of daisies. Josh's family weren't the only Quincys around here, but just in case…

At last, she found Clara's stone. It said only Clara Quincy, Sister and Daughter, and the dates of her birth and death. No one had been here lately. Lydia pulled the weeds and vowed to find out whose job it was to tend this place.

When she finished, she set the vase on the ledge of Clara's stone and poured the water in. Then she added the bouquet. She stood back, and the small grave looked better cared for. Lydia knelt down and flattened her hand to the moist ground. Wind threaded through her hair as she said a quick prayer for Josh's sister and for her own son.

Nothing had changed, except this piece of ground was cleaner. Both children were still gone too soon, but she intended to survive grief and remember what might have been—anticipate what might still be.

She stood up, blinking in the cool air. Time to go back. Face her husband and offer some kind of compromise he could live with, too.

She drove on down the street, purposefully seeking out the high school Josh had attended—looking for some piece of her husband in this town he couldn't love. Instead, she saw two dark-haired boys, bashing at a thick wooden door, which thank goodness, contained no windows.

Lydia stopped the car. "Hey," she yelled.

The boys stopped. Their faces were blurs, but they wore the same sweats. One ran as if she were a minion of the principal's. The other swung the baseball bat at the door again.

"Hey," Lydia shouted again and started searching for a way inside the chain-link fence. The kid bolted. Before she could find an opening, he'd sailed over the top of the fence onto the other side of the wide yard.

Lydia tugged at the links, furious. Kids who vandalized their own school. Who'd they think paid the taxes around here? Their own misguided parents.

In a rage, she dialed Josh. He and Bart must have been too far out. His phone went to voice mail. "It's me," she said. "I'm over by your school and I just saw some kids trying to break in." She turned, scanning the neighborhood, which seemed to be completely empty. Perhaps everyone had run in to hide their heads after she'd started screaming at the vandals. "I suppose I should call the police."

But her anger drained away. The boys hadn't damaged the solid doors, as far as she could see. Besides, she could hardly describe them. Tall, dark-haired, and fast on their feet.

"Call me," she said and hung up. She stared at her phone. A "please" might not have hurt.

She didn't tell Evelyn what she'd seen when she went home. For one thing, she felt guilty. She should have called the police. For another, she felt foolish, having yelled at two boys beating up their own school with a possibly deadly weapon after she'd ranted at Josh for years about his taking chances.

She took a book to bed, but must have fallen asleep. She woke to find Josh easing their door open, a towel draped low across his hips.

"You're awake."

Her glance fell down his body, and he hitched the towel tighter. She blushed. How long since she'd seen him naked?

"What happened?" Though he pretended not to notice, awareness prickled between them. "Did you call the police?"

"No—I know I should have. Do you want to go take a look at the school? They were beating on the doors with a bat. They may have gone back by now."

Surprise lifted his eyebrows. He obviously hadn't forgotten their earlier argument either. "Let's hope not." He took jeans and a sweater from the closet. "Why don't you tell my parents we're going out for a little while?"

"Okay."

He stopped her at the door. "You sure you feel like going out? You're not usually a napper."

"The doctors said I'd be tired for a while."

He let her go. She felt the heat of his fingers on her forearm even as she ran down the stairs.

His mom and dad were chatting in the kitchen.

"There's peanut butter on my paper," Bart said.

"Shh. She'll hear you."

"I love that girl, but have you tried to read through peanut butter?"

"I'm sorry, Bart." Lydia grabbed a napkin and leaned over his shoulder. Finding the offensive spot, she rubbed it clean. "There, and I only got a little of the print."

"Thanks," he said, a laugh in his voice.

"Josh and I are running downtown for a few minutes."

Evelyn looked up from her stewpot. "Now?"

"I have something to show him." That was true enough, and a good way to introduce compromise. "Don't hold dinner, Evelyn."

"The chowder will wait. Josh loves fish chowder." She lifted a spoonful to her lips. "Mmm, so do I." She swallowed in a hurry, blinking at the soup's heat. "This isn't because of Grandma Trudy?"

"Not at all." Hearing Josh on the stairs, Lydia went for their coats in the mudroom. "We'll be back soon."

"Take your time," Bart said with a stifling look at Evelyn.

"Mom, I hope supper won't ruin. Eat without us if you're worried about it." Josh took his coat and put it on.

"We've covered that," Evelyn said. "We'll eat when you get back."

She obviously wanted an explanation but managed not to demand one. Lydia wished they didn't have to be so secretive, but she wanted Josh's advice before she explained what she'd seen to Bart and Evelyn.

In the car, he turned to her. "What happened?"

She told him everything she'd seen, plus thoughts she'd barely acknowledged. "What if it'd been you? You might have been that angry when your parents got out of prison. You could have become violent. But I wouldn't have wanted someone to put you in jail."

In the oncoming gloom of early evening, his eyes seemed darker, wider. "You're usually ready to prosecute."

"Don't make fun of me, Josh. I'm trying to do the right thing."

"But you can't see what it is? Welcome to the real world."

"You're mocking me again."

He laughed, but then drove in silence. At the school, they got out. "I'm going over the fence."

"That's trespassing."

"I can't see from here, Lydia." He glanced around. "Although, I think you were right when you said they'd come back. We probably should call the police." He jumped the fence with as much agility as the boys had and then loped up to the double doors. He tested the surfaces with his hands and then jumped off the porch. If she hadn't known him, she couldn't have made out his face from that distance either.

"I'll look around."

She nodded, her fingers in the links of the fence again. She felt alone, but not uneasy as she waited for Josh to take a turn around the school. He crossed the yard and looked at the fence where the boys had jumped over and then finished a circuit around the building. She backed away as he came closer.

"What do you think?" she asked as he grabbed the top of the fence and swung over.

"They left a few dents in the varnish, but God knows how old those doors are and how deep the varnish goes." He wrapped his arm around her. When she leaned into him, he held on. "I'm surprised you were willing to give them the benefit of the doubt."

"And pleased?" It was obvious in his voice.

"You're not a judgmental woman, but my job has made you less—"

"Sympathetic?" Why not help him? She understood his meaning. "But I've felt as if I were defending myself all this time."

"I see that now."

"Should we call the police?"

"Let's visit. It's a small department, and the chief is a guy I went to school with."

"A friend?"

"Not really. He was a jock. I was a little bit of a pariah."

She grimaced, trying to hide her pain at his matter-of-fact tone. "Okay, but I really do have something to show you first."

"Where?" His gaze hardened. "You haven't been talking real estate with Geraldine Dawson, too?"

"Give me a break. You think I'm that unforgiving?"

He looked guilty. It hurt.

They got into the car. She pointed behind them. "It's the cemetery."

"Oh." He'd probably guessed. "Sorry about that real estate crack."

"It's okay. Who's Geraldine Dawson anyway?"

"A friend of my mother's." At the church, he turned in.

Lydia took his hand as they walked over to the cemetery. He knew the way and she remembered from this morning. He stopped in front of his sister's grave. Lydia would have walked away to give him privacy, but Josh tightened his grip when she tried to free herself. She clung. Somehow this had become a place for their unborn son, too.

At last, he pulled her against him. "Thank you," he said, his chin bumping her head. "She would have liked those flowers."

Lydia nodded, her own throat tight.

"And I like seeing it cared for."

"I said a prayer for her and for our boy."

Josh held her as if he wouldn't ever let her go. "Lydia, I—"

"Don't volunteer something when you're emotional. I know I shouldn't have brought up moving this morning when you were leaving." She cleared her throat. "I don't want to go back to the town house, or to Hartford, but I want to be with you. I'll consider anything you want to try."

"What happened after I left?"

She smiled into his sweater. "Your mom and I talked."

"Again?"

She hardly recognized his gruff tone. "She helped me see what I want—to fight and talk and disagree—and make love again. But real love, not the kind that keeps us limping along to the next crisis."

"What did she say?" He looked as if he were waiting for the other shoe to drop.

"That I'm detached. I never thought of that, but you were busy with a job I hated. I pulled away. I figured you lived your life, and I'd live mine."

"You discussed our marriage with my mother?"

"Stop, Josh. I can feel you getting annoyed.

She said I try to pick the parts of family life I want to be involved in."

"Meaning?"

"I love them. I—" She stopped. She couldn't say she loved him. Not yet. "I'm your wife," she said, "but I try to stay out of the chaos between you."

"It's not your problem."

"If it's yours, it's mine." Instead of welcoming her new commitment, he just stared at her. "Maybe I'm vain, but I thought you'd be happy I want to start over."

"You don't know what it was like to live in this town, with my mother and father. I don't want you to know."

The hints lay in his room. Surrounded by the things Josh had owned at fourteen, she often sensed his pain. He'd never changed anything because he'd never allowed himself to care as much again.

Maybe not even for her. And then their child had died. "Do you blame me for losing our baby?" Looking at him was hard, but she found his tired gaze, fixed on her.

"I've told you I don't." He took her in his arms. His breath rushed across her face. "None of this is your fault."

"I know, but I was his mother. I can't help feeling as if I should have found a way to save him. What made you start distancing yourself before I was pregnant?"

"What?" He tensed.

"Days would pass and we didn't even talk to each other."

"You were in bed by the time I came home from work." He shook his head. "Let's not start that again. We've talked it to death."

"Why did you come back to Maine?"

"For you," he said. "I didn't know it wouldn't be enough."

"I'd move anywhere else. Choose a city with a lower crime rate, a place like this. Give me a chance to protect my children."

"What?"

"The buildings aren't as tall here. Maybe crazy women can't hide behind them."

Saying exactly what she wanted took all her courage. She squeezed her eyes shut, concentrating on Josh's heat in the cool early evening, his heart beating against her ear, his scent spicing each breath she took.

"I won't ever live here," he said. "I don't want to lose you, but I won't lie to you either."

"I don't let myself get attached to this place. I

love the headland, but it reminds you of bad times. Let's sell it and build a house in a smaller town than Hartford."

He pulled away from her. "My grandfather gave me that lot."

"Why don't you resent him?"

"Stop psychoanalyzing me, Lydia. You're an architect, not Sigmund-damn-Freud."

He never swore around her. It was a time-honored Quincy tradition—a practice in control in a home built on disorder.

"He should have stopped your parents before they became—"

"Drunks," he said. "He threw out the bottles they hid in the house and in the barn. He took me out as often as he could find an excuse to. We walked in town or worked in his garden, but he died before Clara was born."

"He should have talked to the authorities."

"How could he betray his own son?"

"Wouldn't you, in the same situation?"

His eyes turned cold and flat—and scared her. They should visit a Sigmund-damn-Freud, someone who didn't care if Josh hated him.

"Yes." He stepped away, staring at Clara's flowers. "But Clara is what bothers me about those years. I'm the one who took care of her, and I'm the one who found her. She needed me. Now my clients need me because I'm not there out of pity—or because I can't get a better job. I try to believe in them."

"I need you," she said. "I'm not a woman who begs or threatens. You know me. You can believe I'm trying hard to save our marriage. I need you more than anyone else does."

She left before he could tell her it didn't matter. He didn't come after her. His lack of action screamed louder than words.

JOSH WATCHED the top of her head as she strode to the car. What was he doing?

He knelt on the wet ground and touched his sister's name, already beginning to weather. He'd been a much better brother to her than he was a husband to Lydia.

Following his wife's lead, he also said a silent word for his son. Standing, he hurried to the car, but once he got there, he hesitated again. A man didn't make a promise under duress that he might renege on when he realized what it cost.

"We have to see the police."

"Okay." Lydia looked out the window.

"You need a decision this second?"

"I need to know what you think."

He laughed and she turned, looking stunned.

"This is funny to you?"

"I was thinking of all those jokes about women asking men what they're thinking." He faced her. "All I can think is that I don't want to lose you, and I need time."

"How much time?"

He started the car. "You're asking me to change jobs and move. Can't you—"

"If you asked me, I'd say yes."

"It's not the same. What if I asked you to stay? What if I said I have to stay in Hartford whether you do or not?"

She dared him with her eyes. "That would be an answer."

"Not the one either of us wants."

He drove to the police station. In front of the square, brick building he reached for her hand. She seemed not to notice.

Inside, they met a woman in a dark-green dress. Kline couldn't afford to use a trained police officer as a dispatcher.

"I'm looking for Simon Chambers," Josh said.

"Do you have an appointment?"

"No, but my wife needs to report an incident she saw this afternoon. Attempted vandalism at the high school."

"Let me get him."

In a second, a tall, blond man walked out of an inner office. Straightening his navy tie, he held out his hand. "Good to see you, Josh. You missed the class reunion last summer."

Josh had spent most of the past fourteen years trying to forget his life in this town, including high school. Right now, he couldn't care less about anything that happened in Kline, Maine.

He smiled in case Simon required the niceties. He'd always put on an act for the people in this town.

"This is my wife, Lydia. Lydia, Simon Chambers."

Simon shook hands with Lydia and then turned to the other woman. "You remember Betty Gaines, Josh? She was a year behind us."

"Hi, Betty."

She grinned. "You don't remember me. I had such a crush on you the summer after sixth grade, and then you went away."

She and Simon exchanged a glance. Simon quickly picked up the uncomfortable slack. "Come into my office. Tell me what you saw, Lydia."

She explained. In the meantime, Betty brought them coffee and a couple of Grandma Trudy's cookies.

"You must love these, Josh."

"I haven't had them in a while." Curious, he unwrapped one and took a bite. Familiar, sweet goodness took him back in time. His mother worked magic with cookie dough. Damn her.

"I probably should have called right away," Lydia was saying, "but I didn't want to cause trouble—"

"You say these boys were both tall and dark-haired. Did they look alike?"

"Alike?" Lydia said, turning to Josh for an explanation.

A little indigestion crawled up his chest. "That's what my mother didn't want to say."

"What are you two talking about?"

"Geraldine Dawson's grandsons?" Josh asked.

Simon nodded. "Geraldine taught us in school, Lydia. The boys' parents left town. She's been trying to raise them, but they're giving her trouble. They're tall and dark-haired."

"I wouldn't know them if you showed me a photo," Lydia said. Her desperate glance brought Josh to her defense.

"She told you what she saw. She has nothing more to say."

"We're not in court, Josh."

"Good, because my wife obviously can't identify these boys for you. Maybe you should put an extra patrol on the school."

"What if I bring the boys by, Lydia?"

"No." She looked appalled, but Josh saw kindness in her eyes. "I didn't see them well enough. Even if I thought they looked familiar, I wouldn't feel right saying so. Add that extra patrol."

Josh stood and this time she put her hand in his. In moments, despite Simon's irritation, they hit the sidewalk. Lydia wrapped her hand around Josh's arm.

"Thanks. I didn't want to get those kids picked up."

"If they try again, he'll arrest them."

"If it was them, but—"

"And they scared you. Aren't you behaving the way you say I would?"

"They're kids. Something's clearly wrong in their lives. It's not as though they killed anyone." Unlike Vivian Durance's husband.

Josh let her go.

CHAPTER SEVEN

AFTER DINNER that night, his mother spread early sketches of the Grandma Trudy wrapper over the living room coffee table. His dad, leaning over her shoulder, pointed at a pseudo-terrifying harridan. "I figured the kids would love this, but the parents would suspect the cookies might be poisonous."

"She is scary." Lydia smiled at his parents, pretending Josh didn't take up space in the room.

His mother laughed self-consciously. "I tried her because we started last Halloween."

"But I thought your mom might make this an ongoing thing, Josh." His dad waved his mug—as he used to wave a half-empty bottle. "Now that people know your product, Ev, maybe we could use that label to promote the Halloween cookie next year."

Lydia bent closer to the drawings. His parents had to realize she was ignoring him. Josh went to the fireplace, grabbed another log out of the wood box and then stoked the fire. He shouldn't have brought up his job earlier. He wasn't trying to prove staying in Hartford was right.

"I thought the business belonged to you, Mom." He glanced at his dad, spoiling for a fight.

"Your father gives good advice, and we like to do things together."

He and Lydia looked at each other. What had they done together in the past year and a half? She didn't know about his cases. He usually knew where she was working, but not what her role was on a project. A man and wife should know more about each other.

Lydia curved her mouth in a half smile that hurt him with its insecurity. How could she doubt he needed her? Her uncertainty made him angry.

"You'd tell me if I was too pushy, Ev?" Bart asked.

Laughing, his mom nudged his dad with her elbow. "Like you'd pay attention."

Josh stared at the fire, an outsider in his child-hood home. His mother and father were the "normal" ones, negotiating a happy marriage. Lydia had all but begged him to meet her halfway, but her idea of halfway and his didn't mesh.

He moved toward her, trying to think of some-thing that would make them talk again. His parents wrapped their arms around each other's waists. Their honest affection stopped him.

How could he show Lydia he still wanted to try without compromising everything he believed in? She wouldn't forgive a lie.

"Mother?" She wanted to use him. He'd use her, too. "I'll help you find a building."

His mother, his father and Lydia all turned with shock that felt exaggerated. Lydia saw him as an unforgiving man. Did his parents view him the same way? He couldn't find a solid spot on this uneven ground. Whether he wanted to get along with his parents or not, Lydia's ultimatum left him little wiggle room.

He turned to business. His career had kept him sane. There, he always knew what to do next. "Why don't you show me your prospects, Mom?"

"Yeah?" She gave a croak of surprise. "Yes," she said in a stronger tone and went back to the desk from which she'd taken the sketches. She drew out several sheets of paper, all well-thumbed.

Returning to the coffee table, she spread out details for several properties. Josh sensed Lydia watching him, but he couldn't look at her. Her response meant too much.

No doubt she'd mention whether helping his mother wasn't enough of a new start.

He started reading the first listing. The words scrambled. He started over. "Barker's Café? When did it close?" On the picture, the windows looked dusty. A faded square remained where the café's name had once hung. The property didn't look tempting.

"Ned Barker left town about a year ago," Bart said.

"Poor Marcy. She came home from work one day last spring and he'd just packed everything and gone." Evelyn expanded on her husband's information, and they nodded in unison. "Marcy's gone to live with their daughter in Phoenix. She'll be warm, if lonely."

"Ned had cabin fever every year," Bart said.

Josh tried not to laugh at the words coming from his father's mouth.

His skepticism annoyed his mother. "You wouldn't think it was funny if you tracked the number of suicides and divorces—even domestic abuse. The longer the winter, the worse the statistics," Evelyn said.

"Are you serious?" Even Lydia, who thought his parents now walked on water, was appalled.

Anything that discouraged her from moving up here worked for him.

"Sounds inviting, doesn't it?" He moved the

Barker pictures and picked up a photo and details for a new building on the same street as the town library.

"I might doubt it, too, if I hadn't lived here all my life. The truth is often all too strange." His mother took Lydia's arm.

"Has anyone compared statistics to cities in warmer places?"

Josh did laugh at last. "Lydia's a scientist at heart." Were they seriously going to discuss cabin fever? With a shock, he realized it was conversation—as any family would make it.

His wife's smile made him wish he could forget fears that were too humiliating to admit. He waved the information for the new building. "How about this one, Mom? The price compares since you don't get the history of Barker's place. Plus, you won't have the upkeep for a hundred-year-old building."

"But we're used to maintaining an old place," Bart said. "Barker's is in a more central location, and she'd inherit their goodwill."

"The newer structure is closer to the docks."

"The working docks, but Barker's is across the street from the boardwalk." Evelyn put the sheet for the café on top. "We'd be closer to the tourists, but the locals are also used to making the trip. I have to give myself the best opportunity."

"Let's consider the rest of these." He shuffled through the sheets, but his mother sniffed. A sound that meant she'd closed the subject.

"I put those two on top because they're the only ones I'm really considering. I like this new building because it's clean and big and has great parking, but I'm leaning toward Barker's."

"Let's make appointments to view them," Lydia suggested. "If there are no problems with this café, and it's the one your mom wants, it sounds like a great option."

"Call tomorrow," Josh said to his mother. "I promised Dad I'd help with the boat again, but we could see them when I get back."

"You're working on a Sunday, Bart?" His mom didn't like that.

"The catch is too good right now, Evelyn. Let it go."

"I'll go with Evelyn tomorrow." Lydia leaned forward. Work distracted her, too. "I can tell her if the structure needs repair."

"Are you ready to take on a day like this?" She was the one his mother should consult. But up here, for this visit, he thought of her as his wife, who needed to recuperate.

"After today? I'm fine."

He might have argued, but anticipation flushed

her cheeks. Sitting back, she folded her hands across her stomach, just happy. No regrets.

"What exactly did you do today?" Bart asked.

Lydia opened her mouth, but then glanced at Josh.

"She cleaned up Clara's grave and took some flowers over. It looks nice." Silence filled the room. "And then she saw two boys trying to break into the school. I'm afraid it might have been Mrs. Dawson's grandsons."

"The twins?" Evelyn grabbed the table. "How did you know it was them, Lydia?"

"I didn't. Josh's policeman friend suggested they were the boys I saw."

"Simon. You remember him, Dad?"

"Sure. He's been a good chief of police. What did you see?"

"Two kids beating on the school doors with a bat. I couldn't say who they were. They were too far away and they ran when I yelled."

"I should call Geraldine." His mother hurried to the hall, her finger on her lips. She paused. "I'll ask her if she minds working on a Sunday and then I'll see what the boys were up to today."

"Mom, I told you—Lydia didn't accuse them. She couldn't really describe them well."

"They've been in some trouble. I didn't want to mention it this morning, because it's Geraldine's business, but I'm worried about her. A woman her age, bringing up troubled young men and starting a new career." His mother kept talking as she went down the hall.

Josh thought of their son with an ache he hid from Lydia. He stacked his mother's pages. "I won't try to persuade you not to go with Mom tomorrow, Lydia," he said, "if you'll come to bed now without a fight."

"I keep going back to bed." But she didn't quarrel. "'Night, Bart." She kissed his dad. "See you in the morning."

"You'd better not. Stay in bed till you wake up on your own." He faced Josh with an old-fashioned father-to-son warning. "You keep quiet when you get up."

"Okay." He looked at Lydia and held his tongue instead of protesting his father's belated protectiveness.

She glanced at him as he eased her toward the hall and then followed her up the stairs.

Halfway up, she leaned back, resting her head against his shoulder for a second. "I know that wasn't just for me, but thanks."

The top of her head was about level with his chin. "It was mostly for you."

On the landing, she looked back, endearingly

self-satisfied. "You made them happy, and I'd like to think I matter that much to you."

"So tonight you don't want to leave me?"

Her expression went blank. "I know you're teasing, but we made a child together. You and I will always be part of each other's lives. The last thing I want is to leave you."

Without letting himself consider consequences, he put his arms around his wife. She stiffened, but she didn't pull away. She had him so off-balance he couldn't be sure he wasn't forcing her.

"Listen to me. I want us to stay together." He fought for the love she'd felt in the beginning. "I want us to be like one of those trees out on the cliff, our branches so bound and twisted, there's no parting us."

Lydia's soft laugh comforted instead of hurting. "Underneath all that anger and bitterness you're a poet."

"I'm trying to work at our marriage, Lydia." Hearing himself, he marveled. "Do you know what it costs me to say those words?"

Even as she smiled, her eyes glistened. "I cry too much these days."

Inordinately happy, he let her go, and she took refuge in the bathroom. In a few seconds, she returned, holding her toothbrush and a tube of toothpaste. "I really am grateful to you for helping Evelyn. She will be, too."

He started turning down the bed. "Don't get all hot about that. What do I know about a cookie store?"

"She wants you for the legal stuff. Negotiating the rent, filing all the correct forms."

"Mom's running a game. She admits it."

Lydia squeezed out toothpaste and began to brush. "You're a service-oriented guy. There's nothing you love more than doing a good deed."

"Thanks. Tonight's diagnosis isn't as impressive when you look all minty and rabid."

She covered her mouth, her eyes smiling over her fingers. "All right—enough marriage and family talk for tonight." She finished her teeth in the bathroom. "I wish you had a television."

"Why?" She watched only old movies at home.

"I'm getting bored lying around. Maybe I'll check out the bookshelves downstairs."

"I'll do it. You've had a hell of a day. Lie down and get a little more bored."

"You don't know what I like."

"Anything with a murder."

"That's right." She pulled a thin, pink band from her pocket and wound her hair into a knot. Tendrils collapsed immediately, but she didn't care. "In fiction, but I like it for the puzzle, not the violence."

"Same as Dad. He'll have something you like."

Downstairs, his parents were in the kitchen. Their voices, friendly and even, almost made him wonder if he'd imagined the brawls of his and Clara's childhood.

In the living room, he took a selection of books off the shelves his grandfather had built to flank the fireplace. He included a P.G. Wodehouse collection of short stories in case Lydia decided murder wasn't her first choice this week.

He was too late. She'd already fallen asleep with her head on the crook of her elbow—on his pillow.

He set the books on the nightstand and pulled the comforter higher the way she liked it. She tunneled deeper.

A rainy gust drew Josh to the windows. Weather rocked the small house as if it were trying to throw it off the cliff. As a child in this room, with a blanket tucked tight beneath his chin, he'd imagined a giant's hand, scooping up the only home he'd known. His parents might have been scary at times, but they'd been more familiar than those unknown demons who'd grabbed at his house in the dark.

Then Clara had come along, and he'd had to look brave to keep her from being frightened. He glanced back at Lydia's still body, grateful for what she'd done for him and his sister today. She was right—she'd given their child a memorial spot as well.

He stared at his own stunned face in the reflective glass. Clara's place had been separate and sacrosanct. Was this what Lydia wanted? To supersede the past?

He drew the curtains to keep out the sun in the morning. Lydia turned, in her sleep moving off his pillow.

He looked over one of the books he'd brought up for her, then dropped it and went to brush his teeth. He changed into clean boxers and returned to his room, yawning after a hard day's labor and an even longer evening, battling with his wife.

As he got into bed, Lydia slid farther toward her edge.

"Hey," he said.

She didn't answer. Her breathing was deep and regular. Even in her sleep she made it clear she didn't want him to touch her.

He turned off the light, suddenly wide awake. He knew how to make things better. But why couldn't she want a man who refused to lie to her?

THE NEXT MORNING, the clock rang—screeched—and then Lydia heard it clatter across the wooden floor. Swearing, Josh pushed himself out of bed and grabbed it. Opening one eye, she watched him fumbling to turn off the alarm.

"Sorry," he said. "I shoved it off the table."

"No problem. I'd have done the same if I could have reached it." Stretching, she reached for him, but he was already gone.

He opened the hall door to let in a little light. "Too much?"

"No." She rolled her head against the pillow, but then turned onto her side. He crossed the hall in a pair of the boxers he'd started using as pajamas since they'd come to Maine. A subtle sign of the distance that remained between them, those shorts irritated her.

He came back, dressed. She must have dozed again.

"I thought you'd be asleep."

"Off and on. I'll make an effort after you leave."

He sat on the bed to tie his sneakers. "These things smell like fish. I'll have to buy new shoes when we get home."

Lydia resisted an urge to remind him Hartford wasn't going to be her home. At least he assumed they'd be somewhere together. "Don't you wear boots on the boat?"

"Water seeps down the sides." He stood, pushing his denim pant legs down. "See you tonight."

"We'll fill you in on the buildings we look at."

He paused at the mirror to push his fingers through his hair. Distance or not, he was still her husband. He still melted her heart with unconscious gestures.

"How good do you have to look before the fish just jump in the boat?" she joked.

Her reflection smiled at her. "When Clara and I were kids, we always wanted to stop at Gordon's for donuts." Lydia froze. He never mentioned tender moments with his sister. "I think my dad's trying to make up for all the times he and Mom were too drunk or too broke to take us. We went to Gordon's yesterday and we're going again today."

"That's nice, Josh."

"It would be if I could forget that Clara won't ever know how hard he's trying."

"Do you feel guilty because you survived?"

Josh turned on her as if with anger. Words didn't come. After a moment, he relaxed and found a smile, both fond and serious at once. "No more analysis, Doctor."

The more they talked, the more they'd resolve, but she had to leave room for Josh's wishes, too. "Okay." She rubbed her eyes. "So, this Gordon guy likes to see your hair tidy?"

"I don't know how long ago the last Gordon worked in that shop. Mrs. Foster, who must be in her seventies, has run the counter since before I was born. She remembers how much I liked apple fritters." He kissed Lydia's forehead and then straightened. Her sense of losing him lifted her hands, but he'd already turned back to the mirror. "Gotta look my best for Mrs. Foster," he said.

"Do you think your father's giving his comb a workout, too?" She tucked the sheet beneath her arms. Josh turned, smiling. "Your mom and I had better make sure Gordon's isn't too near to that shop she wants," Lydia said.

"Come back if you start feeling tired."

She nodded.

He must have seen her. "See you tonight."

"Okay."

In a few minutes, the truck chugged away, but no other noise broke the morning stillness. Evelyn must still be asleep. She'd cooked until almost noon yesterday. Lydia nestled into the warmth on Josh's side of the bed. The man was a virtual heater.

She should get up and start coffee for Evelyn, sneak in a cup of tea for herself, maybe even prepare the fixings for their omelets. She tried to stir, but when had she last been so comfortable?

Next thing she knew, she knew nothing at all.

"DAD, YOU DON'T THINK Mom told Geraldine Dawson it was Lydia who saw those boys?"

They'd stopped for lunch. His father looked up from the most bountiful ham sandwich ever made. "Why?"

"It's the Vivian Durance thing. What if Mrs. Dawson's grandsons were the kids at the school? She might not admit it to Mom, but she might tell them someone had seen them. She might mention Lydia."

Bart cut the engine. "Why don't you call?"

He pulled out his cell phone, but the boat had already taken them out of range. "No service."

His dad tossed the rest of his sandwich to the gulls and went up front to start the engine and take them back toward shore.

"What did Mom tell you last night?"

"She said Geraldine didn't know anything about any trouble at the school. I can't believe your mother would have mentioned Lydia."

"Probably not."

His dad went back to the throttle. "Do you want to go home?"

"No." Before, he would have brushed off any thought of harm coming to Lydia. He couldn't do that now. "I think she'll be all right. Even if it was the Dawson kids, they're just boys."

"With baseball bats." His father started the engine. "But Lydia doesn't like you interfering in her plans."

Josh stared. "What are you talking about?"

"You two live your own lives."

Before Clara's death, no one could have accused his father or mother of being observant. "Because of our work."

"Even when your mother and I were drunks, we shared our sins."

"Just the drinking, right?" Darkness, unaddressed, loomed over his head. He didn't actually want to know more about Bart and Evelyn Quincy.

"This is New England. The variety of sinning I or your mother would dare to do was limited. We had small opportunities. Besides, if I'd ever stepped outside propriety with any other woman, your mother would have used me for lobster bait."

"You were never old-fashioned before, Dad." And Bart's portrayal of Josh's mother wasn't wholly familiar.

"I never let you know me, before. The business was bad. I drank all my fears away." He shook his head. "Which is no excuse. But look, Josh, a taste of old-fashioned marriage wouldn't hurt you or Lydia. You try to manage your ambitions in two powerful jobs. Who's going to give in?"

"How do you know all this?"

"You think we're fools? You're my son, and Lydia is no stranger." He sipped his soda. Ruddy color darkened his rough skin. "And we hear you arguing when you're upstairs. You seem to think the house is soundproofed." He set the can in a holder next to the steering wheel. "Was it when your mother and I quarreled?"

Josh shook his head, fourteen again instead of thirty-two. He'd made up silly games to distract Clara from their loud voices and ugly words. "I'll talk to Lydia. We'll have to keep it down."

"You've said nothing that surprised us. If you don't stop hating us, you'll forget how to love anyone, and I don't say that just for our benefit. I love you, and I want you to have happiness we never gave you." His father cut the motor and lowered his voice and managed to seem less like Dr. Phil. "Try the phone now."

His warning echoed in Josh's ears, along with the dead engine's roar. He couldn't help remembering the millions of promises his parents had made—

"That was the last time I'll take a sip."

"I won't buy another bottle."

"You won't have to pretend we're sick for your sister again."

All in the same tone as "I want you to have happiness we never gave you."

Turning from his father's perfectly sincere face, he dialed home. The phone rang and rang. As did Lydia's cell phone. She hardly ever parted herself from it.

"She's okay, Dad." A massive lump of dread settled in the center of his chest.

"THE STRUCTURE IS SOUND, Evelyn."

"I love this building. I don't even need to look at the others." Evelyn ran her hand fondly across one of the three huge plate glass windows that opened onto the harbor. Even in fall, sailboats whipped across the water, hopping over white foam.

"Wouldn't you love to be out there?" Lydia asked. "Not a care in the world. Just the wind to talk to."

"Maybe for an afternoon." Evelyn stroked the counter, oak, topped by a hundred years' polish and lacquer. "Trust me—no matter how hard you run, your problems wait for you."

"I know." But if she drowned them, it would be out there in the Atlantic.

Geraldine Dawson came up the stairs from the cellar. She'd said nothing about her grandsons. "All dry down there. This close to the water, it's always a worry, but not here. We'd be able to tell if they'd ever had flooding."

Evelyn slapped at a cobweb in the corner of the kitchen doorway. "What is Marcy willing to do about updating these ovens, Geraldine?"

"Not much. She feels you're getting a good enough price that you can replace them."

"I might disagree." Evelyn opened the first one and then let it slam shut, slapping her hands clean. "We definitely need to discuss that."

"How's parking in summer?" Lydia asked.

"Crowded," Geraldine said. "But that's true for all the harbor businesses. Evelyn gets that little paved patch out back. There's room for about five cars, and then three more along the meters in front."

"I'll have to shoo the dive shop customers away." Evelyn checked out the fridge and the cold storage. "I like the freezers. Not that I'll need all that room at first."

"Do you have keys for the other buildings, Geraldine?" Lydia tried to remind her mother-in-law they shouldn't decide without seeing what else was on offer. Josh wouldn't react well to finding out his mother had thrown her bank account at the first property they'd visited.

"I really don't see—" Evelyn said, but Lydia cut her off.

"We need to view them all."

"Certainly." Geraldine fished the keys from the pocket of her rust-colored suit. "I'm yours for the day. Lydia, are you all right to go on with us? I've heard you were ill."

Lydia smiled at Evelyn, grateful she'd kept the facts in their family. People meant well, but she couldn't face the kindness of even strangers until she'd developed a tougher skin. "I'm fine, thanks."

"Are you sure?" Evelyn held the front door while Geraldine checked that they'd locked up out back. "You've slept most of the past few days."

"I'll sit if I'm tired, but you have to promise not to buy something while my back's turned." She nodded toward the storage areas. "What did you tell Geraldine about the boys?"

"Nothing." Evelyn leaned closer. "I asked if she'd heard about trouble at the school. She said no. I couldn't think of a way to ask about the twins without involving you so I dropped it."

Lydia nodded and opened the door as Geraldine came back. They all trooped out in a row.

Evelyn found major problems with all three of the other listings Geraldine showed them. Lydia disagreed with Evelyn's view that the customer area was too small in the newer place over by the fishermen's docks. And the second building did have better parking. She had to admit an electrical fire in a former beauty salon had left water damage and an unattractive odor, but she fell in love with the little cottage that had been an annex to the local Montessori school.

"They didn't have enough students to warrant keeping it open as their administration office," Geraldine said. "Our population is changing and the young people either move the moment they're able, or they've come up here from the cities and then wait to have children."

"Your grandsons live with you, don't they?" Lydia asked. She wrapped her arms around her stomach, not really eager to know if the kind Realtor's grandsons, who were clearly running her ragged, were the boys who'd tried to destroy the school door.

"They're both in high school, both looking to get out of here the second they snatch their diplomas out of Principal Thorne's hand."

"I thought they were still youngsters, Geraldine," said Evelyn.

"The twins are eighteen." The older woman hesitated, her reluctance reminding Lydia she was an outsider. "My daughter and her husband split up. Shouldn't we discuss the Barker café?"

"I like this place, Evelyn." Lydia'd already learned too much. She hoped the boys weren't the ones she'd seen, but who wanted to put two teenagers in jail? "You'd have a guaranteed customer base right next door in the school. One whiff of your cookies and even the parents will pile in for a two-thirty snack. I can see the office walls knocked down. You can put in a new counter like the one at Barker's."

"Or I can use the one at Barker's after I buy the café." Evelyn crossed her arms. "We'll ask Josh and Bart to take the tour, too." She looked over her shoulder. "Although, they're only inspecting here and Barker's. The other places are definitely out." She marched through the cottage's back door.

A talented saleswoman, Geraldine had filled all silences before now, but having confided her family problems, she seemed ill at ease.

"The trees are bare already," Lydia said.

"Our last tourists visit in the fall to see the foliage. Leaf peeping, we call it. The population doubles in size for a few weeks."

Evelyn returned. "You know what I think, Lydia?"

"That this place is a better bargain?"

"It'd make a lovely office for a lawyer." Evelyn slid her fingertips across a desk the school had left behind. "Especially if he wanted to share space with an architect."

"Don't say that." Lydia stared at Geraldine Dawson. She and Evelyn would both be in trouble if that rumor got back to Josh. He really would hate her if he thought she was maneuvering him home to Kline.

Evelyn's knowing nod didn't comfort Lydia. Taking Geraldine's arm, Evelyn led her in low-voiced conversation toward the door.

Lydia followed, but the old school desk drew her fingers to its slick, well-worn surface. She had to stroke the mahogany door frame. The old wood's soft warmth proved irresistible. She could let herself love this building.

CHAPTER EIGHT

As soon as they got home, Lydia layered on sweatshirts and socks and took a book outside to the hammock. Luxuriating in sunlight through the bare oak trees above her head and feet, she had just enough time to wonder when she'd stop keeping a toddler's nap schedule before the book slipped from her hands and disappeared. She fell asleep, trying to convince herself to look for it.

Josh woke her, tucking a quilt around her.

"I'm awake." She tried to sound as if she'd never fallen asleep. Foolish, since he'd obviously been home awhile. The last rays of sun gleamed through water droplets in his hair.

"Sorry," he said.

"No problem." She felt around for her book, luxuriating in the sensuous contrast of cool breeze and the quilt's warm weight. "Did you bring this out?"

"Mom did when she worried you might get cold."

"I may stay here all night. I can't remember when I've been so comfortable."

Affection crinkled his eyes. She savored that, even as she had to ruin it, putting him straight on his mother's plans. "Evelyn's set on Barker's."

"She made that clear last night."

"She's agreed to look at it with you, along with the little school building." Should she tell him what his mother had suggested about their sharing office space? No. She was too toasty and happy. Let him find out for himself that his mother was planning big things for him back in Kline. "What time is it?"

"Just after five. I tried to call you from the boat."

"I wonder if my phone's dead. I don't think I've charged it since we've been here, and I forgot to check messages."

"It doesn't matter as long as you're all right. How do you feel?" He leaned against the tree at the end of the hammock. One hip jutted as he braced his foot against the trunk.

"Fine." Too fine, looking at him. She knew the lanky body he took for granted as if it were her own. She'd taken comfort in him as she took comfort from the warm embrace of her mother-in-law's hammock and quilt. Sometimes marriage could be that basic.

"Why did you try to call me?" she asked.

"I wasn't sure what my mother said to Mrs. Dawson."

"About me? I wondered that, too." She smiled, warmer than ever. "I'm glad you worried, but your mom was discreet."

Putting both hands in his pockets, he rocked against the tree trunk. "I've always worried. Ever since the first threat, I don't mention you at the office," he said. "Your name isn't in my paperwork. I don't even list you beside my emergency number."

"Why didn't you tell me? I would have felt better."

"I didn't know I had to." He straightened. "You think you're out of my head the second I leave home in the mornings? You're my wife."

"I am your wife, but I need a little more information about where we stand."

"You mean where we're going?"

She nodded. "I'm trying to be patient."

He pushed away from the tree and knelt beside her. She held out her hand, and he kissed her palm and then rested his cheek against it. "Will we be all right?"

"I want more than all right." She wriggled closer. "Before, I settled for 'all right,' but we're both frozen inside our doubts. We need true love we can trust to make a marriage. We deserve that kind of love."

Behind them, the mudroom door opened. He looked up. "Give us a minute, Mom."

After a second, the door closed again.

He kissed her, hard and fast, a man claiming his wife. "I want the same things you do." His strong tone broke the hard shell Lydia had tried to form as he'd faded to the edges of her life. Every part of this man meant too much to her. "I'm even trying with my mother and father because of you. Maybe the baby and my parents and—Clara— they're all mixed up in my mind. I don't know what comes next, but I won't let you walk away."

Walking was the last thing she wanted. "I'm not going unless you force me." She could have trusted him. She could have admitted she still loved him. Hardly believing happiness could be so close, she held back with the part of her that disengaged for safety.

She clambered out of the quilt, but faltered, her muscles protesting as she stood. "After a few days of lying around, I'm out of shape."

"What do you mean?" He ran his hands over her, as if searching for an injury.

"I'm achy." Shivering in the crisp air, she locked her arms around Josh's neck and pressed her lips to his in a chaste promise to start over. Passion, they understood. They needed deeper feelings that couldn't burn themselves out or freeze in a nuclear winter of grief for their lost child.

He caught her close, his breathing swift. "I've missed you."

"Me, too."

He fingered her hair away from her ear and kissed the base of her throat. "We'd better go inside. My mother will think we're in a heated battle."

He reached for the quilt. She took the other end. Together, they folded it. Each time their fingers met, his warmth made her want to follow the quilt into Josh's arms.

If he'd hated losing her, too, why had they stopped talking? Distance had grown between them as naturally as choking weeds in an unkempt garden.

Josh opened the kitchen door. "Here we are, Mom."

Lydia slipped past, brushing his waist with her hand. Her nerve endings were sensitized, her awareness of him almost painful.

His mother looked up from a half-made salad. Spaghetti sauce bubbled on the gas range. A loaf of Italian bread waited on the counter between crushed garlic on a cutting board and a mound of freshly grated parmesan cheese.

Warm light filled the kitchen. Good smells and

the signs of people living life reminded Lydia she was also alive. "I'm starving, Evelyn."

"Supper's almost ready. Your father's back from the hardware store, Josh. I wonder if you'd help him unload paint from the truck."

"Paint?"

Lydia looked up. "I thought you worked together on the boat today. What's your dad doing at the hardware store?"

"He went out again while I was in the shower." He went to the counter and snagged a grape tomato, which he popped into his mouth. "What's he up to, Mom?"

"He thought you might like to help paint the barn."

"Like to?" He stared at his mother. "Have you noticed how big that barn is? Some chat over a few cans of paint isn't going to make us move back here."

Lydia laughed. "You're in danger of overplaying your hand, Evelyn."

"What's funny? You don't realize it, but Bart's getting older each day. He can't do everything by himself."

Lydia worried a little about her father-in-law, who was only in his midfifties. Josh laughed out loud. "Mom, he could whip my ass in a fight."

"Josh." His mother pretended to be shocked.

"Okay—I give up." Josh shot Lydia a look of surrender. "I'm dying to paint the barn." Passing Lydia the quilt, he headed out to help his dad.

Evelyn scooped the quilt out of Lydia's arms. "Am I clever, or what?"

"Or what, I'm thinking. He knows exactly what you're up to."

"He's never been so wild to help around here before." Evidently feeling she'd maligned Josh, she continued. "Not that he's lazy, but he never hangs around long enough."

"I know." Lydia had been along for every visit in the past five years. She knew this family's construction as well as any of the buildings she'd worked on in Hartford.

"You agree he's weakening?"

He was making different choices to save himself from his own bitterness. "There are four sides to the barn, Evelyn. How do you know they won't split them up?"

"Spoilsport. Bart will make sure it all goes according to plan."

"Stop trying to manipulate Josh. He deserves better."

"We all deserve better."

"He won't come home to stay." And yet,

Kline felt more like home to her every time she came here.

"We'll see." Evelyn pointed her toward a stack of plates and silver and carefully folded, snowy linen napkins. "Feel like setting the table?"

"MAYBE LYDIA'S right, Bart." Evelyn turned from the dressing table, rubbing lotion on her face. "I should stop manipulating our son."

"Try to keep your voice down, honey. One thing we've learned from this visit is that they can hear every word we say."

Evelyn shared a warm smile with Bart and wished Josh and Lydia could find the trust she and Bart had struggled so hard to achieve. Unequivocal. No matter what he said or thought, she knew he'd be on her side. And he could assume the same about her. "Josh guessed what I was up to that first day they were here." She looked up, rubbing the last of her moisturizer into her elbows. "They seemed better together tonight."

He laid his book flat on his chest and took off his reading glasses. "They were more comfortable together. Isn't that more important than what we want, honey? Josh and Lydia are getting along again. Let's leave them alone to work out their problems."

"He's going to help you paint."

"I don't need to paint already. You're getting desperate."

"Yeah, I panicked. Lydia was so energetic today, I suddenly thought they might go home and we'd sink back into an armed truce with Josh."

"We can't make him change. I've gone along with you so far, but let's try being honest. We just want our son to be part of our family. We don't have to trick him. Tricking him won't work."

"Neither has being honest all these years. I don't understand why he's chosen to help, knowing I was working him." She came to the bed and pounded her pillow. "He's seen the barn, and he's a country boy at heart. He has to know the paint's only a couple of years old."

"Our tricks have nothing to do with it," Bart said, gentling his tone. "He's lost a son. He and Lydia are apparently a lot closer to separating than we ever dreamed. Family gets more precious when you know what you're giving up."

"I know—believe me—I know, but I think it's more. Whatever they're fighting about includes us. Every time I try to get information from Lydia, she clams up about Josh, but you can bet he wouldn't be here if Lydia hadn't pushed him to come."

"Give up for tonight, Ev. Just come to bed." He set his book on the nightstand.

Evelyn lifted the bedding and burrowed into his side. "You're so warm."

"And I'm right about Josh. Don't push him anymore. Let him decide what he wants from us."

"I think it's working, though."

"Evelyn."

"All right, but I like making things happen, rather than waiting."

"Feels as if you have more control?" he asked.

"Are you saying we don't?" Bart was usually the more sensitive, though he'd never brag about it. She tended to barge into a situation and hope for the best. Impulse control, her therapist had called it all those years ago.

"The kids could leave tomorrow. I don't want a relationship with Josh because he's staying for Lydia, or you've talked him into helping me paint."

"All right. I'll leave him alone, but is it okay if I still ask him to look at the properties with me?"

"Yes, honey. Just don't talk him into anything else he doesn't want to do."

He turned off the light. Evelyn welcomed his arms around her. Often in the night, she remembered how it had been to sleep without him for almost two full years—grieving for their daughter, longing for their son, who was being worked to death on a dairy farm. All because of the things she and Bart had done.

"You'd think guilt would have made us hate each other after what happened," she said.

"Who else could we talk to about it? Anyone else would have blamed us as much as we did. No one else could have felt how deeply sorry we were—and how afraid for Josh."

"I love you, Bart, and I'm going to trust your instincts about him."

He kissed the top of her head. "I'm going to hope your trust is well-placed."

THE NEXT MORNING, Lydia was watching the morning news when a story came on about the science lab at the high school burning.

She stood, knocking her plate of eggs to the floor. "Josh?"

"Huh?" Surrounded by real estate papers, he hadn't been paying attention until he'd heard the plate fall.

"The school. Someone did break in last night."

"How do you know?"

"Look, look." She turned his mother's small television in his direction and then wiped up the eggs. A man in a suit was talking about storms offshore raising the tide.

Josh lifted his papers in an unspoken "what?"

"They'll talk about it again. What if it was those boys?"

"They've graduated to more dangerous crimes, and Simon has a problem on his hands."

"I mean what if they were Geraldine's grandsons?"

"Could you have identified them?"

"I told you I didn't see their faces clearly. Maybe if someone put them in the same clothes and made them run across the field."

"Which Simon would never do." Josh concentrated on his paperwork again. "You did your duty."

"Why do I feel guilty?"

"Because you don't want to see young boys in trouble, but you wonder if you should have done more."

"Who's Sigmund-damn-Freud now?"

"What do you want to do, Lydia?"

"I'm thinking of calling Simon."

"Well, I won't let him put Mrs. Dawson's grandsons in a run-across-the-field lineup for you. Why are you smiling at me?"

"Because you call her Mrs. Dawson as if you were still in high school."

"Time in this town stopped for me the day I left for college."

"She's been awfully nice to your mother, Josh. You wouldn't believe how difficult Evelyn was yesterday."

"I know what I want," Evelyn said from the doorway, "and I don't see why I should waste Geraldine's time or mine, looking anywhere else."

"Because you can't make a purchase like this with your heart first, Mom."

"I'm putting your father's and my money into this building and this business. If my heart isn't there, we'll both be in trouble."

Lydia only half paid attention to their wrangling. "I'm going over there."

"Over where?" Josh and Evelyn asked in one voice.

"To the school. The fire trucks are still there. The school's closed. Maybe those boys I saw will be there and I'll recognize them."

"What are you talking about?" Evelyn asked.

"Someone broke into the high school and burned the lab."

"The whole lab?"

"I don't know, but they talked about extensive damage."

"You can't accuse Geraldine's grandsons without proof."

"I've been bending over backward to avoid doing that, Evelyn, but this is serious."

"You don't know they were even the kids you saw." She grabbed a mug from the counter. "Let me have one cup of coffee and I'll come with you."

"I'm taking a shower and getting dressed. If you want to go, you'll have to be ready when I am."

"Wait," Josh said, "I don't want them seeing you if they did something and they think you might identify them."

"You're the one who said they were kids."

"I was wrong," he said. "Don't go over there."

"I'm going."

"Mom, if you want to come along, be ready when we are," Josh said.

Lydia couldn't believe his sudden loss of common sense. "Let's take the circus over. Your mom's fine, Josh, but everyone in this town knows you're an attorney. If they see you, they could think I'm out to get them."

"Why are you going?"

"I just want to know what's happening. Evelyn?"

She pulled the cup away from her mouth and waved her hand in front of her lips. "I'm burning myself to hurry. Give me a second. Josh, I think she's right."

He stared at them, but Lydia could tell he was thinking something more than "why can't I make them do what I want them to?" He suddenly stacked the papers on the table in front of him. "I need to speak with Mrs. Dawson."

"About her boys?" Evelyn set her mug down. "You can't do that."

"About your real estate ambitions. I need to know about deeds and title searches. You know how confused those things can be in a town like this." New England property turnover could be as twisted as the lines of history and family marriage. "If she happens to mention the boys came in smelling like gas, or covered in soot, that's none of my doing, but no, I'm not going to interrogate her."

"Oh, like she'll do that." Laughing in utter relief, Evelyn pushed Lydia toward the hall. "Get dressed before your husband does something crazy."

"They'll think Mom's there to help you finger them," Josh called.

"Josh, no one uses 'finger,' anymore. I watch the movies."

Lydia laughed at Evelyn's patient tone, but Evelyn poked her in the back.

"I think you're foolish to do this. I'm only coming with you because someone's going to have to hold those boys off you if they did this and they think you know."

"I wasn't at the school last night. I know nothing about the fire."

"That will make all the difference to two teenage boys who are furious because their parents apparently didn't want them so they beat up a door with a bat—and then—for all we know, set the place on fire."

"Don't scare me." Lydia didn't want the boys to be guilty, but she couldn't help wondering if she might have been able to recognize them. A little better than she'd claimed.

Juries had to be sure. Shouldn't a possible witness be, as well? If someone had made a guess about what Vivian Durance was going to do and said nothing, Lydia would have considered that person as guilty as Vivian.

WHAT KIND OF IDIOT let his wife march into danger because she felt guilty for doing too much and not doing enough all at the same time?

"Damn," Josh muttered at the television. "Who gives a—who cares about the freakin' corn queen of Iowa this morning?"

Specialty features, one after another, including a fascinating story about a garden hose that wouldn't freeze, even in a Maine winter, paraded across the screen.

"What's up, Josh?"

His father hadn't ever slept so late. At least not that Josh knew. "Someone burned the school science lab, and Mom and Lydia have turned into vigilantes."

His dad yanked the television to face him. "You saw them on here?"

"No, before they left. They wouldn't let me go with them."

"Let you? Are you out of your mind?" His dad's hands were already at the tie to his robe.

"Wait. They were right. Two women, milling in the crowd aren't as threatening as even one man. If you and I go down there, eyeing the Dawson twins as if they were Frank and Jesse James, Lydia could look like a witness."

"So we wait here?"

"As long as we can stand it."

"Let's paint the barn."

Josh swallowed his frustration. "This is one time when work won't distract us, Dad. I'll call Mrs. Dawson."

"And ask her if the boys—"

"No, to talk to her about Mom's building." Josh

pulled a sheet of notes toward him and then stood up to get the phone.

"You're willing to let your mother and Lydia wander around in that mob," he pointed to a shot of the school, complete with fire trucks and anxious parents and students, "without either of us to protect them?"

"You think there aren't cops in that crowd?"

His dad leaned in, to see the picture better. "I don't see Simon. Wait, there was a patrol car."

"Dad, I'm worried. It's irrational, but considering what happened before..."

He dialed Geraldine's number. It rang and rang and rang. And then it rang some more.

"She's not home." He eyed his father as he hung up the phone. "Doesn't mean she's at the jail, right?"

"I don't care if we have to put on false beards. I want to make sure my wife is safe."

His father's panic heightened Josh's. He'd been sensible before, and Lydia had gotten hurt.

"Come on, Dad. We won't let Mom or Lydia or anyone else see us."

THEY WERE EVEN wearing the same clothes they'd worn the day they'd tried to beat the door in. Twin boys, as tall and as dark-haired as those boys had been on Saturday, hovered at the edges of the crowd.

Lydia didn't have to ask if they were the Dawsons. She pretended she hadn't seen them at all.

"Recognize anyone, Lydia?"

She jumped. Simon Chambers had surfaced at her elbow. He walked like a spy. The better to catch recalcitrant teenagers or unwilling witnesses, she supposed.

"Do you have someone in mind?"

"Since I don't have proof, I won't taint the process, but you have to admit this isn't a coincidence."

"Yeah."

"What are you saying to my daughter-in-law, Simon?"

"Not a thing, Evelyn. What are you doing here? You're not Lydia's watchdog?"

Evelyn laughed. Lydia had to force herself not to gape in awe. The world had been robbed of a high caliber actress.

"Look at me," Evelyn said, emphasizing her smallness. "She'd be better off with a puppy."

"You'll let me know if you see anyone who disturbs you," Simon said.

"Sure." Lydia borrowed some of Evelyn's skill. "You'll let me know if you have any proof before you have me identify a suspect?"

"You've been hanging out with Josh for too long."

"Thanks."

"I'm going to visit Mrs. Dawson."

"You leave her alone," Evelyn said, breaking character.

Simon searched her face. He glanced at Lydia, who tried not to look as shocked as she felt at Evelyn's aggression.

"My turn to thank you," he said to Evelyn.

He faded into the crowd. Evelyn grabbed Lydia's arm. "What did I do?"

"You just took up for a friend."

"And put her in the police frame."

"They're not going to frame Geraldine or anyone else."

"I guess—I don't trust them."

"I can understand."

"Let's go see her, too."

"She might not be home," Evelyn said. "Would you wait around in your house for the cops to come get you if you thought your grandsons might be responsible for a crime like this?"

"I don't know. I don't even know what I should do." Lydia turned toward the square. "Let's walk down there. Maybe we'll find Geraldine doing some business research."

Before they'd gone far, she spied Josh, a head

taller than the men around him, hanging back on a corner near the church. About ten feet away, his father was trying to blend into a telephone pole.

CHAPTER NINE

"EVELYN, we've been followed."

"Huh? The cops?"

"Worse. Husbands."

"Where?"

Lydia nodded. "Toward the church. They're obviously trying to look inconspicuous."

Evelyn laughed out loud. "They worried about us. Don't laugh when we get to them. They can help us look for Geraldine. She may need Josh anyway if those boys have been up to no good."

"For once the idea of Josh defending someone doesn't turn my stomach."

"Did you see them back there at the school?"

"See who?" Lydia asked blandly.

Evelyn didn't bother to answer.

THEY DIDN'T FIND Mrs. Dawson on the square. She wasn't in her office. She didn't answer her home phone. Josh suggested they might be overreacting, and they finally gave up. After lunch in a lobster roll shop, they went back out to the house. Josh and his dad tried to clean the kitchen they'd left filthy, but his mom pushed them out. She liked having things done her way.

Afterward, she suggested Lydia might like to learn her cookie recipe. Lydia jumped at the chance.

More of his mother's plan? To show him his wife, all fifties homemakerish, churning cookie dough in a massive bowl?

"Dad, that barn's waiting for a coat of paint."

"It'll wait until tomorrow."

"Isn't that why we decided not to take the boat out today?"

"Yeah." His dad was the son, being dragged to an onerous task.

Josh was already up a ladder, applying paint, when his father showed up. "When are you going to get sprayers, Dad?"

"When I don't like to take a week to do the job right."

"You don't know how to use a sprayer, do you?"

"No, and I don't want to learn." Another ladder banged against the wall beside Josh. "What's got you up here slapping my barn as if you're on a vendetta?"

"Just getting the job done. Lydia's doing pretty well. We may go home soon."

"Home?"

"To figure out where we're going next."

"Son, are you quitting your job?"

His father should not be the first person he told. Lydia must already know he wouldn't let her leave him over a job. But she didn't know he could be wholehearted in his need to be with her.

"I'd rather talk about the barn, Dad. I don't think I have the patience for one more lecture."

"Some people don't look on paternal advice as a lecture."

"I do."

"Then let me point out, you're skipping spots on my barn."

"Good tip."

He painted better and faster, frustrated with himself for giving in, but more because he'd been truly afraid for Lydia this morning. All those years she'd worried about him—about them—was this how she'd felt?

"Are we racing?" his father asked after about half an hour.

"I don't know what you're talking about." But they hardly spoke and they finished one end of the barn by dark.

Josh's arm ached as he helped his father clean the brushes. "You know, this is a waste of time. How many catches are you handing off to some other guy while you're on a ladder? A sprayer would get you back to work in record time."

"We did all right, and I like the process of it. You can see where you've been, where you're going, what you've accomplished." His dad washed his hands one last time and patted Josh's shoulder with more force than Josh could have done with. "And my son and I accomplished painting one whole end of this barn that's been in our family for over a hundred years."

"This building?"

Bart nodded. "I don't mind admitting I'm a romantic. I like the history. I love the continuity of doing this with you."

Josh wanted to be like his father. It was one of the strangest, strongest moments of his life. "Dad, I have to finish here. Could you ask Lydia to come out?"

"Sure."

In a few minutes, Lydia slipped inside the double doors at the other end of the barn and hurried toward him. "What's wrong?"

It wasn't like her to expect the worst. Time to try to help her change their lives for the better. "I wanted to talk to you."

"You're sick of painting barns and catching fish and strolling Kline streets?" She paused for a breath. "You want to go back to Hartford?"

He wiped his hands and arms on one of his father's scratchy "work" towels and threw it into a hamper beneath the sink. "No," he said. "I want to find a new place to live, somewhere you can be happy and I can still find challenges in my job without frightening you."

Lydia's eyes widened. She curved her mouth in half a smile, but then looked serious again. At last, she sagged against the stool at his father's workbench. "What?"

"When you left today, I knew you were safe. Deep down, I don't believe two boys—or any boys would hurt a grown woman who happened to pass by a school when they were doing something they shouldn't."

"What if they torched it?"

He stopped. "You saw them?"

"I may have seen the boys from Saturday. They were twins, and they were hanging around the school today."

"That doesn't make them guilty."

"No," she agreed. "But it doesn't clear them either. Why did all this change your mind about Hartford?"

"I thought I was being paranoid. I was so worried about you I couldn't concentrate on anything else. I got a taste of how you felt. I'm sorry I couldn't just see what you were trying to tell me. Apparently, I'm a thoughtless clod who had to be in the same situation before I could understand."

"But you do understand?"

"You haven't changed your mind, Lydia?"

"I'd never set foot in that town house again if I could avoid it."

"I'll take care of selling it."

"I'm not letting you do all the work," she said and suddenly she sprang off the stool and wrapped herself around him. "We're getting out of there?"

When he'd finally left the foster care system, he'd sworn he'd never run scared from anyone or anything again. But he'd run to keep Lydia safe. Staring into her eyes, feeling as if parts of himself were disappearing, he set her back on the stool.

"Josh." She held on as if they'd both fly apart, into the air if she let go.

With a finger beneath her chin, he raised her face. Her mouth opened with anticipation. He knew it from her quickened breathing, the deep light in her eyes. He kissed her. He claimed her back from darkness and fear that had taken her away from him.

She kissed him as she hadn't in years, with passion and certainty—not a desperate need to forget—that he only now recognized.

At last, he let her go and they clung to each other, breathing hard.

"That's been a long time coming." Lydia grinned. "I have to call the office and tell them I won't be coming back—make sure they can find someone to take my place."

He laughed, surprised at such an unexpected store of happiness. "I can't believe leaving will be so easy for you, but I'm glad we're going to be okay," he said in the soft strands of her hair.

A noise roused him. A car, approaching at speed on the gravel driveway before he'd had time to remind her he was still going to be a defense attorney. Easing away from Lydia, Josh leaned into the nearest window. "I'm not that surprised. It's the police."

Lydia slid off the stool and almost fell. He caught her.

"Don't be afraid," he said. "Unless they found fingerprints on an accelerant, they were bound to be suspicious of two boys who've apparently done small things like rolling the courthouse lawn and soaping all the police patrol cars before now. Simon has to wonder if they've graduated to breaking into their school."

"Oh my God, and all because I went to the police."

"I thought you weren't sure enough to identify them, Lydia?"

"The boys I saw today had on the same clothes as the kids I saw Saturday." She turned toward the doors. "Do I have to talk to them?"

"If you don't, it'll look worse for the Dawsons. Just tell the truth."

"Most of the kids in this town probably have those same high school sweats."

"High school sweats?" Josh pushed her toward the door. "I'd even advise you to think twice before you identify someone based on the sweats they all wear if they're in organized sports."

"I'm not trying to get them off, Josh, even though I am thinking of what could happen to their family if the police take them in for this. Geraldine seems so fragile. It wouldn't take much to hurt her badly."

"Getting them off wouldn't help them," he said. "If they're the ones, they have to make some kind of reparations. But I can see you're worried they are guilty, even if you're not positive. Knowing Geraldine shouldn't change your decision to speak up or be cautious."

"Okay." She started toward the doors. "I'll talk to them."

Simon was coming to the barn as Lydia opened the door. "What's going on?" he asked.

"Nothing. How about with you?"

"I'd like to talk to you." He held out his hand to Josh. "Good to see you."

Josh acted as if he was just as pleased to see his old schoolmate. "Come inside. Mom always has a fresh pot of coffee."

Lydia was glad to stand back as he led the way to the mudroom door. Josh caught her hand at the steps.

"It's going to be fine. Tell him what you believe. Just don't lie."

She veered her glance upward.

He grinned. "I've never known you to lie. Let's move it before they think we're out here talking over your testimony."

"Easy for you to make light. You're not on the verge of ruining some kids' lives."

"They probably beat on a door. That won't ruin their lives."

Simon looked up from stirring the coffee Evelyn had put before him at the counter. "Glad you two could join us."

"Come on, Simon. My wife never deals much with the police. She told you she'd seen a problem, and now you're here to question her when she doesn't know anything about that fire last night."

"We're not in court, Josh."

"Fire away, Simon." Lydia went to a seat across from Josh at the table. She didn't want to seem as if she needed his backup.

"Did you see the boys from Saturday by the school today, Lydia?"

She resisted a strong urge to look at Josh or his mother. This family—her family—had suffered before and after the system took over and tried to correct the problems in this house. Josh's life with his foster family loomed uppermost.

"If I were positive I wouldn't hesitate to say so. I saw a lot of boys who looked like the ones I saw on Saturday, but no one I could point out to you without a shadow of a doubt."

"That's the standard for a jury in a murder trial. I'm looking for suspects in a school arson case."

"I can't help you," she said.

"This is a small town. I've already had to talk to them about some *cute* things they'd done," Simon said. "Even I can see the humor in soaping patrol cars, but burning down the school…"

"Even if they were the ones who tried to break in, I can't say a thing about this fire." Lydia did glance at Josh. Deep in his eyes she saw admiration. "I wasn't at the school last night."

"I just want to talk to them, Lydia. They may not be the ones. You might be helping me clear them."

"I can't do anything for you."

Josh stood. "I'll walk you to your car, Simon."

"Just a minute." Simon sipped his coffee, offering Lydia plenty of time for second thoughts. "How are you going to feel if you don't tell me the truth about these kids, and they hurt someone with their next so-called prank? You can see they're getting more dangerous."

"I'd feel sick with guilt, but I'd feel worse if I chose two boys who looked sort of like the ones I saw, and they got in trouble because of something I said, but they were innocent."

Simon picked up the cap he'd hooked on the back of a chair. "I guess I can't argue with that." He put on his cap. "Even if I want to. Remember this is a small town and we have our share of gossips who've heard what you saw."

"Are you threatening my wife, Simon?"

"I don't want either one of you to feel unwelcome."

Josh gestured toward the door. Simon left without saying anything else. Josh followed him out. Lydia felt uneasy.

"One good thing's come of this," Evelyn said. "You look at Josh as if he matters again."

Lydia and Josh had yet to agree on the details of what they actually wanted, but he'd given her new hope for the first time. "He always mattered," she said, "but I like having him in my corner." It was that simple. He could say he wanted to save their marriage till doomsday, but today he'd acted to keep them together.

The door opened and Josh came back. Without thinking, Lydia ran to him, pulling herself as close as she could—until her heart beat against him and his was a pulse against her cheek.

"What?" He held her so tightly she could hardly breathe.

"I'm happy."

Wrapping her hair around his hand, he gently tugged her head back. "Because of me?"

"Absolutely." She remembered his parents behind them and turned. "Oh, they're gone."

"Fled at the first public display of affection," Josh said and leaned down to display a little more.

The phone rang behind them. Lydia glanced at it. Josh let her go.

"Maybe we should go upstairs."

His mother swept into the room, looking anywhere but at them. "Sorry," she said. "There's only this one and the one in our bedroom." She snatched up the receiver and said hello. "Geral-

dine." She sagged against the counter. "No. Nothing's wrong." She straightened, a flush of red on
her cheeks. "There is with you?" She listened a
moment and then looked at Josh. "No, I don't
know anything about it. Lydia saw some boys by
the school, but she's never said they were Mitch
and Luke. She insists she can't identify the young
men she saw."

Lydia felt a little sick. Josh wrapped his arms
around her waist.

"Well, I have to ask if you still want to help me
out, Geraldine." Evelyn looked even more taken
aback at the other woman's answer. "I'll ask my son.
Maybe we'll all come for a second look." She held
her arm way out so she could read her wristwatch.
"Seven-thirty tomorrow morning? Okay. See you
there. I'll call you if we can't make it." She hung up
as Bart entered the room behind her. "We have to
think hard about this property question. Someone
has put in an offer on the Barkers' building."

Only Bart spoke. "Did she say anything about
Lydia?"

"Oh, yes. She asked if the rumors were true,
that Lydia had seen some boys vandalizing the
school on Saturday and said they were the twins."

"And you said?" Bart prompted.

"You have to ask? I told her Lydia couldn't

identify anyone. Now will you all come with me in the morning?"

"Mother," Josh said, "I'd rather Lydia didn't go."

"I'd just as soon not go in the morning if people are gossiping," Lydia said, her mind on Josh's history of feeling like a town spectacle. "You go with your mother."

Evelyn ran a hand through her hair. "I want that place, Josh, but I'm willing to listen to reason if you have any. Otherwise, I'll ask Geraldine to bid on my behalf."

"I'm not a real estate attorney. I can only tell you whether I think it's worth the money or not, and what does my opinion matter?"

"Your father and I have looked at it many times. Lydia's seen it. Your opinion's important to me even if I'm prepared to disagree. I admit I'm doing this with more emotion than business sense, but I'd like to know what you think."

"I'll be around here all day," Bart said, "even though there's nothing to worry about. Lydia, you can keep me company while I paint."

"Dad, you're not putting her on one of those stepladders."

"I didn't say that." Bart looked insulted. "You stand in that café window and look out at the boardwalk and the water and the crowds of people down there even on a Tuesday when the season is virtually over, and then tell your mother it's not the prime spot in town."

Josh turned to Lydia, but she shook her head, trying to tell him she'd be fine with Bart. "I can't help factoring in the money."

"I've discussed the financials with the other business owners along the harbor," Evelyn said. "They make the bulk of their profit while the tourists are here, from spring until the end of leaf-peeping season. I'm better off if I'm right there in the customers' faces."

Lydia wanted Josh to go. "I'm not worried, and there's no reason for you to be either. You should see the café since it means so much to your mom."

Josh gave in. "What time, Mother?"

"I'll knock on your door when my alarm goes off. I can't help wondering if we're going to be too late. Geraldine told me the dive shop on the other side is looking to expand. They want to connect the buildings."

"They can't put anything through tonight," Bart said. "The kids must be hungry. What do you all say to breakfast for dinner? I make a mean pancake."

"I'll do the bacon," Josh said.

"We have some maple syrup." Evelyn turned to the cellar. "I used it in some cookies the other day.

Ruined the recipe, but I wanted to try something new." Her voice faded as she went down the stairs.

Bart grinned after her. Josh glanced from his father to Lydia with a smile. And she felt like part of a family.

Later that night, she slept in her husband's arms and felt like a wife.

RAIN THE NEXT MORNING made painting impossible. After Josh and Evelyn left, Lydia and Bart shared kitchen duties. Twirling the tea towel, Bart looked for another dish to dry.

"I think that's all," Lydia said, rinsing the sink. "Evelyn couldn't have done better herself."

"But we won't mention it. How about a game of cards?"

He surprised her. "Sure."

"I'll set up the table in the living room."

"I'll make fresh coffee. If another cup won't bother you." Evelyn had mentioned cholesterol. She hadn't said a word about hypertension.

"Caffeine has no effect on me," he said. "It was my lifeline after—for a while."

She understood. He'd switched from liquor to coffee. While she worked in the kitchen, Bart banged around in the living room. As the coffee's aroma wafted through the house, he returned, sniffing.

"Mmm. Smells perfect. Evelyn never makes it strong enough." He took out his favorite mug and poured himself a liberal dose. "You're joining me?"

"But I'm corrupting the elixir with milk and sugar."

He gave her a formal nod. "You're only a woman."

"And we all have our rituals," she said.

He'd opened all the curtains in the living room and started a fire that chased back the cold. No one could mask the sound of the ocean, licking at the cliffs. Salt scented the air, whipped by the sea, into the wind.

"How can Josh turn his back on this place?" Sitting at a card table, with coffee in front of her, Lydia stared at water streaming down the windows, at the gray sky boiling beyond.

"You know the answer."

Clara filled the silence.

"What made you go clean Clara's grave and put on fresh flowers?"

"I did it for Josh, to remind him he had nice times with her, too. He's eaten up with guilt."

"I'd take that away from him if I could, Lydia. God knows his mother and I carry around enough for a mob. None of it was his fault."

"But he'd managed to help her so many times.

I get the impression he tried to make her think you all were sick, rather than—"

"Drunk. You don't have to be polite. Josh has plenty of reason to rage at the bad times that never should have happened to either of them. But memories of the good moments just make him miss her more."

"Again, because he feels responsible. If he saved her from realizing how bad things were, he thinks he should have saved her life."

"Probably the key to all our problems, but he refused to see a counselor—figured he could get over it on his own, and he's never turned to us. He refuses to believe this is his home—and even back then, we would have defended him or Clara with our lives—if only we'd known."

Lydia stared at her coffee cup. It swam in front of her. She blinked hard, but finally gave in and brushed tears from her eyes. "Have you ever said exactly that to him?"

"I try to tell him every time he stays long enough to hear me out." Bart shuffled cards whose backs were faded almost white. "So not too often. And maybe not in those words."

"You should try," Lydia said. "I used to think he'd get over the past and we'd move here."

"Maybe some day." He turned away, setting

down the cards, and peered through the curtains. A lull in the rain let him see the land he loved and the ocean beyond. "Everyday, I wake up and wish I could change the moment my daughter died. Then I pray my son will want to be my son again."

She started to go to him, but he glanced back, Yankee repression in his eyes and she stayed in her chair. "How do you give up almost two decades of anger that's made you successful and safer than you ever were before?"

"Hasn't that attitude made problems for your marriage?"

"I've already talked too much about my marriage. Josh likes privacy, and I've developed a big mouth."

"Let me just say this. Work has been his penance. You're his reward."

"I don't want to be some payoff when he has time to pay attention." She lowered her voice. "Besides, he's going to switch jobs."

"That won't matter until you make him realize you come before work." He shrugged. "Not that we've been good at dragging him back into a family life. Maybe you should think about another baby."

Guilt at saying too much turned into resentment. "You think our unborn son would be so easy to replace?" With her last strand of control, she kept from reminding him no little girls ran around this property.

"I'm sorry." Bart came back to the table. "Sometimes I talk too much, too, but I keep thinking if you two solve your problems, mine with Josh will all work themselves out. I didn't mean to intrude, and you're right. No child is replaceable." He stared at her, a hard stranger who wore the face of Josh's tenderhearted father. "I want my son to come home, and I hoped you'd make him realize family is more important than any job, any house in a strange town. He has no reason to prove his worth to people who don't love him."

"I can't discuss this with you, Bart." She dropped the cards and stood.

He took her arm. "Does this place feel like home to you?"

A few days here had changed her, too. She'd become softer. Kline was the place she'd choose to live and make a family with Josh. The headland felt like home. None of which she could say—because she had to prove her loyalty to Josh.

"I enjoy visiting you and Evelyn."

He grunted, dissatisfied.

She turned toward the hall. "I'm going to find a book and lie down, Bart." She should have kept her mouth shut. She prayed he wouldn't interrogate Josh about changing his job.

He'd work in any courthouse in the country before he'd take a position in Kline.

Bart's harsh mood had reminded her she and Josh had settled nothing. One thing was certain. Josh would never agree to come home to Maine.

CHAPTER TEN

JOSH VAGUELY REMEMBERED Geraldine Dawson. Hair the color of copper and a too-bright sales-woman's voice. She'd always tried to make calculus sound like a win-win deal.

"How are you?" Her handshake was firm. Worry lines were new.

"Fine." He couldn't help studying her for clues of her troubles at home. "How are you, Mrs. Dawson?"

"We're all old enough for you to call me Ger-aldine." She held out the keys to his mother. "Thanks for coming so early. I know it's an impo-sition, but I didn't want someone else to rob you of this opportunity."

His mother opened the door like a woman who already owned the place.

"Mom, wait." He had to make her see facts. "Think about the consequences. Naturally, Mrs. Dawson wants to sell the place. Sorry," he said.

"Geraldine," she said again. "And I don't blame

you, but I believe the feeling one gets in a building is important. Evelyn senses that this place is right for her business."

His mother urged him through the door first. "See how you feel, Josh. If you like that other building better, we'll talk. But this is cozy. My customers will want cookies and cakes and tea and hot cocoa."

"And coffee," Geraldine said. "I'd kill for a cup of coffee."

She distracted Josh, and he glanced at his mother to find her staring at her Realtor friend as well.

"Have the police been bothering you, Geraldine?" she asked.

The other woman gathered her composure. "Not about the fire. They can't with no proof, but you know how this town is. People think Luke and Mitch are guilty and they've made sure I know it." Her false laugh might have shattered glass. Josh wanted to reassure her about Lydia, but she looked away.

Inside, the wooden floor creaked. His feet still knew which boards made the noises in this little café. The wooden display cabinets still shone, red-brown. Three plate glass windows, though dusty, displayed the harbor like three wide, fine paintings of the sea no human with a brush could ever match.

"I see what you mean, Mom."

"Goodwill is worth the price."

"Shouldn't we look at the other building, though?" He turned to her friend. "Mrs.—Geraldine, you brought the other keys?"

"I've seen enough," his mother said. "If you feel the way I do just walking in, that firms up my decision. Geraldine, I need some advice on the bid."

"I'm not sure what the other party offered." A phone trilled from inside Geraldine's purse. "Excuse me. The boys—" She grimaced at Josh as she opened her phone. "You won't be surprised to hear I wish they behaved as well as you did."

His mother led him to the kitchen as Geraldine spoke to her caller. "We may have to update next year, but for now, these stoves are adequate."

He ran his hand over the scratched metal. "I guess you know what equipment you'll need?"

"I've been baking cookies for years. These ovens will give me a huge step up compared to the one at home."

"Have you thought about staff?"

"I figure I'll hire maybe a high school student at first, to man the counter while I'm back here. I'll have to do as much of my cooking as I can in the evenings." She opened a mammoth fridge that smelled a little musty. "We'll need some baking soda." She sounded efficient.

"Why didn't I ever know this side of you?"

"Until Clara died, I'm not sure I knew this side of me. Afterward, you didn't want to know."

Well-nurtured anger flooded back in a poisonous stream. "How can you say it so matter-of-factly?"

"Practice." Her deep breath didn't manage to hide a battle against crying. He knew that feeling too well. "I was in therapy for years. I haven't gotten used to it or accepted it. I've learned to talk about it."

He stared at her thin, lined face and wouldn't let himself pass judgment. For a change. Love waited in her eyes, waited for him to hit at her as he always had.

"I know what you mean," he said instead. "We never saw our son, and we didn't give him a name, but he was as real to us as if he'd been born. I feel cheated. At least Lydia held him in a way. I never got to."

Grief broke the last words in his mouth. His mother came to his side.

"Josh," she said but waited for him to give her some sign of his feelings.

The animosity of decades paralyzed him, but

Lydia was right about his family. In the end everyone needed a mother and father. They'd all suffered enough. He held out his arms and his mother walked into them. She was so small she reminded him of Clara.

"I'm sorry about the baby," she said. "I'd do anything to help you and Lydia."

"Lydia and I have to help ourselves."

"Marriage is compromise."

"Mother," he glanced toward the other room, where Geraldine's voice was rising, "I want to make a new start with you and Dad, but you can't advise Lydia and me."

"Whatever you say." She ducked into a huge cupboard. "I was startled to hear Geraldine say you behaved well in school. I imagined you were a bit of a tearaway."

"Because I couldn't get along with you and Dad at home, school was a relief."

She shut the cupboard door, her face drained of emotion. "At least you're honest."

Hurting her was too easy. "Maybe I don't always have to be." He wished he could take it back. "I still smell fresh-baked bread in here."

"I know, and it's still making me hungry."

The door squeaked. Geraldine came through. "Evelyn, I'm sorry. I have to go. I'll call and let

Marcy Barker know to expect a bid. Then I'll call you later, and we'll discuss price. Don't worry. They won't accept the other buyer yet." She nodded at Josh. "Nice to see you again."

She left in a rush, leaving her keys behind. He grabbed them from the counter where his mother had laid them.

"I'll return these."

He caught Geraldine on the sidewalk. She was searching her purse, her hands frantic and shaking. "Oh, thanks." She shut her purse and headed for a dark-blue car at the curb. "Just turn the lock and pull the door shut when you leave. I'll come by later and set the alarm."

"Okay." He wanted to ask her what had happened, if her grandsons were in trouble again. But he thought of how Lydia would react if he volunteered his services. "Drive carefully," Josh said, feeling ridiculous. The woman looked as if she might fall apart.

"Thanks. It's a relief seeing you. I'm going to remember that troubled young men can become responsible citizens." She opened her car door. "But damn it, you were determined and self-directed. My boys are—oh, never mind."

He tried to let her go, but he'd seen too many people in her state of despair. He and his own sister had been as frightened. And no one had come to their rescue. "Can I help you?"

She shook her head, her mouth tight. He watched her get into her car. She had to know someone trustworthy who could help her. He hadn't come here to fix anything except his marriage.

But she backed away and he felt as if he were deserting a woman in need.

"You know those grandsons of hers are in trouble again."

His mother stood at his elbow.

"I think so, too."

"I thought you might offer to talk to them."

"I considered, but I'm here for Lydia." He looked back at the café. "Did you lock the door?"

"Yeah, but I hated to leave. It feels like my place already." She went to his car. "Maybe I should suggest Geraldine talk to an attorney here in town."

"That would be a good idea, Mom, but first she has to admit something's wrong."

"That's a problem."

"While you try to solve it, let's go by the court-house and see what we can find out about the title to Barker's café. I'd like to know if there've been any disputes over the property in the past."

"And you thought I was just using you."

"Don't kid yourself. A title search is expensive. You're getting a bargain in me."

RAINS CAME AGAIN the next day. Lydia woke to find Josh dressing, not in jeans and his paint-spattered shirt, but in a suit.

"I didn't know you brought that," she said.

He turned, knotting his tie. "I made an appointment to talk to Brice."

She sat up, tucking the sheets around herself. "Why do you need to talk to your boss?"

Josh came to the bed. "To tell him I'm quitting," he said. "Don't worry. I'm not backing down."

"I didn't doubt you."

"Sure you did, but I don't blame you."

She pulled his hand to her cheek, trying to believe in this more attentive, forgiving version of Josh. "You're going to stay this way even if we work things out and stay together?"

He stepped back. "I thought we'd already agreed to stay together and work things out."

"Try not to get angry." So uncertain of each other, they were both touchy. "I'm afraid."

"You won't ever have to be again."

She tugged him down and brushed his lips with her fingers. "I'm afraid of losing you."

"You won't ever have to be again." He opened

her mouth with his, and she tasted his toothpaste. She tasted passion that felt new and wondrous, but too fragile.

"I'd better go." He rose, his eyes disturbed, his breathing rushed. "Take it easy today."

"You, too."

He shut the door and she laughed. Only two people who cared deeply about each other could be so inane.

THE DRIVE to Hartford took less time than usual. Josh found Brice and Brenda in his office, already going through the files.

As soon as Brice saw him, he signaled for Brenda to return to her office. He sat in Josh's chair, leaving the client's chair for Josh.

"Morning," Brice said.

"You've been busy."

"You wanted this to go fast."

The faster the better. He felt a certain amount of guilt. "I'd like to finish off the cases that are close to trial."

"I'm glad to hear it. You don't want to hear you're making a mistake?"

"I'm not."

"Who made you an offer? Which firm finally lured you out of here?"

"I don't have another job. I told you the truth. I'm leaving because Lydia doesn't feel safe anymore, and I'd like to make a fresh start with her in a place that doesn't have our memories here."

"We caught the woman."

"Brice, has the job made you cold-blooded? Nothing the D.A. could ever do to Vivian Durance would make Lydia forget what happened. Why do I have to tell you that?"

"Because what happened is a shame, but it's part of life. Are you going to run every time your wife gets spooked?"

"I'm going to do what it takes to make my wife happy." He felt like an idiot saying it, but maybe this was his penance for taking her for granted.

"You'd better straighten out your priorities, buddy."

"I have." Now that felt good. He'd been a job-first kind of guy—so much so that Brice Dean felt comfortable treating him as a like-minded clod. Now he was a husband, and someday, he'd be a father. Josh reached for the top file on the teetering pile. "Might as well start with this one."

Lydia found a sketchpad deep in Josh's closet. She would have preferred graph paper, but this would do. In the kitchen she rummaged through the drawers until she found a pencil with a good eraser.

Fortified by a cup of cocoa and an unexpected sunny splash of late-afternoon heat on the kitchen table, she began to sketch. A house. The home she'd dreamed of all her life.

Three fireplaces—the predictable one in the family room—but Lydia added another in the kitchen and a last one in the main bedroom. She could imagine that room, large enough for the oversized, antique bed she'd found before she'd ever met Josh. They'd paint the walls a soft, warm blue and add pale drapes that offered privacy but never blocked out the sun or moonlight.

She gave in to the ideas flooding her, an office for Josh, a sewing room for her, bookshelves built into the walls on a large landing with room for two fat chairs and a table between them.

A playroom for the children she still longed for. A home that would keep her family close.

As she pushed the pad away to admire her work, reality stepped in. Dreaming might be a mistake. She and Josh still hadn't discussed the future, but she'd walked the newly mown headland, clothed in an old raincoat and happiness after Josh left to resign.

Walking on the headland always gave her ideas about what could be. She'd fended them off in the past, knowing Josh would never consider inhabiting a "compound" with his parents.

But today, so close to freedom from fear and memories that hurt too much to contemplate, she couldn't resist an act of optimism. And no one ever had to know about her daydream.

The house continued to appear, as if she'd been drawing it in her head for years. She had. A Cape Cod, bigger than this one, modified to include four bedrooms, because she and Josh had always talked about a large family. And those children would always want a home to return to.

"Nice."

She jumped, and Bart put his hand on her shoulder. "I'm sorry. I didn't mean to scare you, but I've never seen an architect work."

"This isn't a blueprint, just a few sketches." She sipped her cocoa. "I thought you were on the boat."

"I came back early. The benefit of being your own boss. No word from Josh yet?"

"Did you expect him to call? He has a lot of cases to turn over to Dean." She sat straighter. "You're not going out there to paint alone?"

"No. It's too late, and with all this rain, I'm thinking of hiring a guy who knows how to use a sprayer anyway. I need to work on the boat for a few days in a row." He peered around the room as if he could see through walls and ceilings. "Evelyn's not home yet either?"

She'd left just after lunch. "I haven't heard from her. I think she's still trying to get information out of Geraldine, but Geraldine's afraid of me."

"You went for a walk in the rain?"

"I was restless." She couldn't tell him she was celebrating.

Smiling, Bart turned the notepad. "I can see this on the headland."

"Me, too." But Josh wouldn't share their enthusiasm.

"I won't tell Josh."

She shut the pad. "You know him too well."

"I do." He sat in the chair opposite hers and reached across the table to pat her hand. "I'm sorry I was so cranky last night. I get that way when I'm worried. If it's any consolation, I probably owe my son an apology, too."

"That's family, I guess, taking it out on each other. We're all tense." She set her pencil beside the paper.

"Does Josh know about that at all?" He pointed.

She searched for a flip answer. None came. She wanted to live in a place like his hometown, and she was beginning to want it too much. "He has no idea."

"He has a right to know what you want." Suddenly impatient with himself, Bart pushed back his chair. "Here I go again, beating you about the head and shoulders with so-called wisdom. I don't like apologizing so I'm going out to the barn. I can usually find some work out there."

"Forget it, Bart. I don't always mind advice." She went to the fridge. "I should see what we have for dinner. Josh and Evelyn may be out all day."

"He wants your marriage to work. Do you know how much he loves you?"

She started, vaguely aware of a lettuce leaf hanging over the crisper drawer and a small dish of sour cream rocking, because she'd jerked her hand away at Bart's declaration. She should know how Josh felt. His quitting was a message she needed, but she still needed more. "You're doing it again." She tried to make a joke.

"It wasn't advice—more a statement of fact my son doesn't seem capable of making."

How could Bart and Evelyn be so sure of Josh's feelings? "Look—pork chops."

"And it's obviously what you need to hear more than anything else."

His interference shocked her. She didn't see Bart thinking so deeply about his son and her and their marriage. And she didn't want him saying such things to Josh. This was her battle—with her husband. For once, she was the one who'd resent his parents if they didn't stop trying to help so much.

Bart saw her impatience. "I'll be outside. That should keep me from talking."

"I'm not asking you to go away," she said, "just to give us room."

"And I'm trying to tell you that you're as much my daughter as Josh is my son. Evelyn and I love you both. Spending so much time together, I thought I could tell you."

She touched his shoulder. "You didn't have to. I've always known." She turned away, self-conscious. "You want to help me with dinner?" She opened the crisper and found carrots and celery, broccoli and onions and two different kinds of squash. "If I chop up these vegetables, will you grill them, Bart? Oh, look, there's an eggplant, too."

"I'll chop. You sit. Josh and Evelyn won't like me putting you to work in the kitchen." He scooped the vegetables out of her arms and laid them on the counter behind a large blue cutting board.

"I'm fine, and there's room for both of us."

Bart lit the grill outside and ran back in, shivering. "Man, it's turned cold out there."

"Too cold? I can stir fry."

"I'll put on a jacket. Let me run up and get one that doesn't smell like fish. Josh likes grilled, and Evelyn may have something to celebrate. Let's give them both a treat."

As he went upstairs, Lydia glanced at the clock and considered calling Josh. He was probably stuck in traffic. And Evelyn—she must be negotiating the real estate contract of a lifetime.

Bart came back down, his thermal shirtsleeves rolled up, prepared to work. He draped his coat over a chair. He and Lydia were chopping in companionable silence when the front door opened and Josh and his mother came in.

"You've been together?" Bart asked.

Lydia studied her husband's face for some hint of Brice Dean's response. What if he'd managed to persuade Josh to stay?

"We met outside," Evelyn said.

Josh took in the scene, her working beside his father. He snatched a piece of broccoli and crunched it between his teeth. "What's going on here? I know it's trite, but you two make me wish I had a camera."

Lydia nudged Bart. "I was hoping to hear a little sarcasm when they came back, weren't you?" She glanced at Josh, impatient for a clue. "So I started this and then I put your dad to work."

He laughed. Evelyn took his coat out of his hand. "I've hardly ever managed to. Put Bart together with the kitchen tools, I mean. Not that he doesn't have a talent." Evelyn hung the coats in the mudroom. "You'd better get used to this, Bart. You'll have to help if you want to eat once I'm working out of the house."

"Did you get the building?" Lydia had caught Evelyn's excitement over the business and the café.

"I'll know tonight or tomorrow." She rested her hand on her tall husband's neck and tugged him down for a kiss. "So you'd better fit yourself for a manly apron."

Josh laughed. "Won't the rubber one he uses on the boat work?"

"He's not bringing that thing in my house," Evelyn said. "Mmm, what are we doing here?"

Josh washed his hands and then drew a knife out of the block and nudged Lydia. "Out of my way. I'll take over."

"If I can traipse all over town, I'm fine to chop a few vegetables, assuming I don't add my inexpert fingers to the mix. Evelyn, we're having grilled vegetables and pork chops and jasmine rice."

"How'd it go in town?" Bart asked.

Thank God someone had. She was so eager, she'd dreaded looking triumphant.

Josh slotted his knife into the eggplant. "Fine. No problems, though I don't have an end date yet." He looked at Lydia. "We should have talked this over, but I'd like to finish the cases I've brought to trial."

"I understand that. You can't walk out on those clients. But what happened? Was Brice upset?"

"He wasn't pleased." Josh sliced the eggplant without looking up. "He suggested I should straighten out my priorities."

"Your priori—" She broke off, full of righteous indignation. "Isn't that what I was begging you to do as well?"

"Bart, we should—find somewhere else to be," Evelyn said.

"No, Mother, it's okay." Josh whacked away on the eggplant and reached for another, imperturbable. "I told him I had set my priorities, and we went through my caseload."

"And that's it?" Lydia asked, not daring to believe.

"I quit my job. We have to decide where we're going next. We're starting completely over." The phone rang behind them. "If that's Brice, I'm busy."

Lydia laughed. "So he's not letting you go without a fight?"

"He said I'd be hearing from him as he went through my notes."

"I'll tell him you're not home yet." Evelyn picked up the receiver. "Hello?"

"I didn't ask you to lie, Mother," Josh said.

She waved him off. "Simon, she already told you she didn't see those boys well enough to know—" She turned away. "And I'm afraid you can't insist. Josh knows our rights."

She started to hang up the phone. Before Lydia's eyes, Josh turned into what he was, a defense attorney with an eye for the big picture. He caught his mother's arm.

"Don't. It's a game." He took the phone. "What do you need, Simon?" He listened for a moment, and a frown creased a line above his nose. "How many of them? All the way down the boardwalk?" He nodded. "Not at all. She's never even met them." Another silence. "Okay, we'll come over, but I don't expect Lydia will give you a different answer just because you show her the boys up close."

He put the phone back. His gaze wary, he faced Lydia. "I'm afraid if you don't go down there now, he'll think you're trying to hide something. He asked me how well you know Mitch and Luke."

"I'm starting to get sick of their names." She ran her hands under the water in the sink. "Or, rather, what I may be forced to say about them."

"No." Josh washed his hands, too. "If you don't

feel certain, you stick to your guns. You can't identify them."

"I know."

He turned to his mother. "I don't know when we'll be back. Don't wait on dinner."

"Shouldn't we go with you?"

Josh grinned. "Lydia's capable of telling the truth without a posse behind her, Mom."

"I'm not talking breaking her out of jail. I'm suggesting family support."

"That would look ludicrous," Bart said. "I'm sorry you've gotten involved in this, Lydia. It's obviously unsettling."

"But probably a beneficial lesson in what Josh faces everyday." Lydia dried her hands and dragged her fingers through her hair. "I'm ready. What is Simon looking to pin on those kids now?"

"You're suspicious." Josh stood back for her at the mudroom door. She grabbed her coat, and he helped her on with it. "Someone hammered all the parking meters on the boardwalk last night. He thinks with a baseball bat."

"Wood against metal? Seems like much ado about nothing."

"Metal and glass," Josh said. "Some of the meters lost the battle, and the bat seems like the Dawsons' weapon of choice if they're the ones you saw."

"I'm dreading this."

"This is nothing. Either you know it's them, or you don't."

He kept repeating it, but she needed to keep hearing she didn't have to guess.

At the police station, Simon met them at the door. He came down the front steps. "We're not a high-tech department. We don't have a two-way mirror, so you're going to walk into a room and take a look at Luke and Mitch and tell me if they could be the boys you saw."

"Look at them. My God, how is that going to make them feel?"

"My question, exactly," Josh said. "They're just kids."

"They're eighteen. If they want the fun of destroying property, they can take the consequences. I know you're sensitive to kids from a broken home, Josh, but we have to stop this problem before they do something serious. And I still don't have anyone else in mind for the school fire."

"So why not accuse two troubled kids?" Josh put his arm around Lydia's shoulder. "I'm familiar with the process."

"Why are you both so determined these two are innocent if you've never met them?"

"I didn't come up here to put children in jail,"

Lydia said. "And being eighteen doesn't always mean a kid's suddenly an adult overnight."

"They certainly don't show an adult's judgment."

"Enough." Josh held the door for Lydia. "Let's get this over with."

Everyone in the building, including a man with a mop and pail, eyed Lydia as if she were a criminal. Josh's tension seeped into her shoulder. She suddenly understood his reluctance for small-town familiarity. Why couldn't these kids cut out the fun and pranks?

Simon opened a door and suddenly, she was in a windowless room, faced with two lanky, dark-haired boys who stood on either end of a long, gray table. They presented mirror images of each other, except for the grimace on one adolescent face, and the contempt on the other.

"Where's their grandmother?" Josh asked.

"Eighteen," Simon said again.

Josh looked annoyed. Lydia stared at the boys—who stared back. She wanted to warn the scared one not to look so frightened. Simon seemed in the mood to take fear for guilt.

"I'm sorry," she said. "They—" Josh, apparently realizing what she was about to say, instantly stiffened beside her. "The ones I saw were so far away, their faces were blurry. They were tall, but

I don't know how tall. I can't say these are the *children* I saw."

"These *young men* are doing all right by you," Simon said.

"You're stepping over the line," Josh said.

"I'm angry when any kids are so mad at their home situations they take it out on property that belongs to everyone in this town."

"Well, we aren't the ones," the angry boy said. "Can we go now?"

"Sit down." Simon stared at Lydia.

She said nothing else. He gestured toward the door and she and Josh went out again. Simon followed them.

"You seem to have a grudge against them," Lydia said.

"They've been causing trouble for over a year. I'm worried they'll go so far I won't be able to help them," he said. "If they didn't set the school on fire, I'm not looking for jail time for these boys. Geraldine loves them, but she can't control them. I have access to agencies that might be able to help them."

"Yeah," Josh said. "I've been the victim of that kind of help."

"That was eighteen years ago. Times have changed."

"Call us if you need us, Simon. Good to see you." Josh shook hands. Lydia let him steer her toward the front door. "I can't believe he made you go in there. It wasn't fair to them or to you."

"I know you and your parents don't trust the system, but maybe we should assume Simon's telling the truth about his intentions."

"He can have the best intentions in the world, but those kids are better off with a grandmother who loves them than they'd be in a system that sees them as a file number. And they are eighteen. Simon might lose control of the process."

Outside, he pulled her close and glanced behind them to see if anyone was close enough to hear. "Did you recognize them?"

"They looked familiar, but I still would have said they were the ones if I'd been sure."

"Okay," Josh said.

"I can't believe you had to ask that."

It was his turn to grimace. "I won't deny I usually deal with people who aren't afraid of shading the truth." He took a second look at her. "You weren't afraid of them?"

"They're not exactly scary." They waited for a patrol car to pass between them and their car. Icy wind slipped into the open lapels of her coat. She parted from him to go around to the passenger side. "Although I may be confusing them with you, so they stop looking like the boys I saw."

Josh signaled for her to get in. She followed.

"Don't say that." He leaned across the seat. "I don't want you to feel sorry for me, and I don't want you to confuse actual kiddy criminals for me. If they're doing the petty crimes, they need some help."

"But not to do the time?"

"I'd have them spearing garbage off the sides of the road from Nova Scotia to New York."

She pulled the seat belt halfway across her lap, but leaned back. "I'm exhausted."

Josh fastened it. "My job looks different from here?"

"It does," she said. "And I only have to consider Geraldine, not small children or a wife who might be expecting a new baby."

"Or fathers and mothers dependent on your client's meager livelihood—or merely the fact that your client looks guilty to the cops so you have to prove innocence when the prosecution is supposed to prove guilt."

"I think that is happening here. Simon seems certain."

"I have a bad feeling about the one on the right side of that table, but maybe I'd be aggressive, too, if someone assumed I'd turned into an arsonist."

Lydia closed her eyes. "I can't believe this still goes on, two kids painted with scarlet letters."

"Don't you love this town, though?"

"Gloating is never attractive, Josh."

"Do you still want to live here?"

She'd lied about that for years, to save her marriage. "Yes," she said, looking into his appalled eyes, "I do."

CHAPTER ELEVEN

SOMETHING PLINKED against the window. Josh moved closer. Minuscule light streaks shone on the darkness in the glass. "It's snowing."

"Your dad said it was cold outside." His mother, wearing reading glasses, glanced up from her embroidery frame. "Do you miss our early snows?"

He looked at Lydia. Sprawled on the floor, she looked so focused on her book, she might not have heard his mother's question. She'd dropped her bomb in the car and abandoned it as it lay between them. Apparently, it was up to him to explode.

"It snows in Connecticut too, Mom."

"And that snow's better in some way?"

"It comes without the things I don't like about Kline."

"What would be so wrong with living here?" Evelyn lumbered on where Lydia had halted on the precipice. "This is a great place to raise children. Young couples like you move up here all the time."

Josh stared from his mother to his wife. Lydia hadn't turned a page in awhile.

Unbelievable. "Are you nuts?"

"I might be a little, but we've come so far," his mom said, an octave higher as she realized her mistake. "You own land here. You have family."

"Evelyn, this is the wrong time."

"Thanks, Dad, but I can't believe I have to tell any of you that no amount of time will change what happened here." Lydia, from the floor, leaned on one elbow to look up at him. "I don't know if you and my parents have been planning this, but you'd all better realize I'm not moving back to Kline."

He stood and went to the kitchen, and then to the mudroom, his only thought to get out of the small house that sucked his soul. But there, he hesitated. Lydia would follow, and she didn't need a stroll in the snow.

She'd often said she felt trapped in the town house in Hartford, but his wife knew nothing about being caged. He paced to the front door, which came too soon, and then he turned into the living room, which was untouched, but pristine. No one used a living room in Kline, Maine, unless the minister or the mayor dropped by.

"Josh?"

"Try not to sound afraid of me, Lydia."

Her hand on his arm, she turned him. He expected an apology. She'd broken their unspoken agreement. A home in Kline was off-limits. But her hard gaze startled and held him. "I am not afraid of you. I have never been afraid that you'd do anything that would hurt me."

"Other than keep the job that made me who I was."

"Who you *were?*" Unease laced her tone. "You'll be another man somewhere else?"

"I don't know who I am when I let an aberration in one woman's behavior chase me out of the town and the job I love—where I made a difference, Lydia."

"Are you talking about me or Vivian Durance when you say aberration?"

Good God. He eyed her without bothering to answer.

"You're angry because I wanted you to quit?"

"Let's not talk blame," he said.

"If you do blame me, we should. How can our marriage survive if you're keeping a quiet grudge?"

"I didn't want you to leave me." That mattered most right now. "I did what I had to do to make something right."

"I wanted to come before your clients. I didn't want to live in a place and a house that hold such horrible memories." She blushed. "I know that's what you'd be doing if we moved here, so as much as I want to live here, near your parents, on the headland you already own, I'm not asking you to do that."

"I got angry because I felt pressure from you and my mother. Dad tells me what to do all the time, but at least he leaves me alone to make my own decisions." He stroked the back of her neck, trying to comfort with actions, since he couldn't find the right words. "I care more about what you think than anyone else, but we can't say anything new about this."

"Shouldn't talking help?" Lydia asked. "I'm trying to reach you. You obviously want to be with me. Why can't we say the right things?"

"We don't know them?"

She seemed to look inside herself. "That leaves us nowhere. How do we learn what to do to keep each other happy? Where do we turn?" As if she knew there was no answer, she left the one sterile, unfriendly room in Evelyn Quincy's home and climbed the stairs. "I'm going to bed, Josh. I'm not angry."

He wanted to go after her, but she was right. They

could talk about Mitch and Luke Dawson, Clara, his job and the holes in a system that made children victims twice over when their families fell apart. But eventually, he and Lydia had to stop thinking about Hartford or the Kline police or his past.

They had to face each other.

And when they tried, they seemed to find silence instead of a future.

"Don't pretend your problems will get better if you leave them alone."

"Mother," he said without turning, "this is between Lydia and me."

"I know what I'm talking about."

He stared her down. "Yeah?"

"Your father and I had problems. Haven't you ever wondered why I drank?"

Hell, yes. He turned so fast he nearly knocked her over. "Why?"

"I was a horrible mother. I didn't feel the usual bond, though I prayed to." Tears filled her eyes. If they hadn't, he might have hated her. "You needed me and I was frustrated by everything I had to do for you. It never seemed like enough. And yet I loved you. I wanted to be the mom you needed—like other moms. If I drank, I didn't feel as much—emptiness. And then when you were eight, Clara came along. Same thing. I was bad. Bad all over. What woman feels impatient rather than maternal? And how could I resent the time I had to spend buried in this house—" He eyed her sharply. She broke off.

"I'm sorry. The walls just closed in on me. I had a life so many women wanted. I could be home and raise my babies, no day care, about enough money to get by, but I was smothering in Dr. Seuss and corduroy jumpers, Little League practice and play dates where all the other women talked about their joy in the things that frustrated me. I felt like a leper in this little stuck-in-the-TV-fifties town. Maybe if I'd worked outside—no, forget it. That's the past," she said.

"Mom." She'd listed his worst fears. "I'm thirty-two, but I don't want to hear raising me drove you to drink."

"It didn't." She took his hands. It was all he could do not to shove her away. "I'm trying to tell you my failings drove me to drink. I should have admitted I needed outside work, too. I should have found a way to be happy at home. I love you, son, and I still want to be your mother."

"That's some kind of love."

She flinched. He hardly noticed, didn't want to care. "You felt this way about Clara, too?"

She recoiled. "I only realized what I was rejecting when I couldn't have you anymore. I didn't care what anyone in this town thought of me after that. I only sat in that cell and cursed myself for every moment I'd thrown away, every instant of happiness I could have given you or Clara, with just a little less despair, a little more acceptance. Something outside that damn bottle would have made life easier for all of us."

"Did you ever tell Dad?"

"No. And maybe that kept us both drinking. I was ashamed, and I thought Bart could only love me if he drank enough to dull my complaints. We never actually addressed our problems. We both tried to drown them."

"He's no saint in this."

"We didn't go straight to a therapist for marriage help back then. We were fools." She looked tired, used up by the past and her dissatisfaction and the harsh climate of their hometown.

"Why didn't you start this Grandma Trudy business then? Maybe you'd have liked coming home if you'd had other work to challenge you during the day."

"After I came home from—prison—I tried to make up for the past. I made myself into June Cleaver, but you no longer cared. After all these years, I began to feel pointless again. I—" She licked her lips. "You probably don't understand. I still dream of the taste, the cool fire—you look horrified, Josh."

"Because I'm seeing my sister face down in that green pool."

"Son." She caught him close. Her slender arms were steel. Her tears wet his shirt. "I can never tell you how sorry I am. It has no end. I'd give my own life for my little girl's. I don't even know if she knew I loved her."

Josh couldn't speak. He just held on.

After a few moments, his mother pulled back, wiping her eyes with her fists. "I started Grandma Trudy's because otherwise I'd have started drinking again."

"It helps?" he asked, and he cared about her answer.

"I love the challenge, even when I'm afraid I'm cooking us into the poorhouse. But it doesn't make up for Clara." She tiptoed to kiss his cheek. For the first time in eighteen years, he didn't step away. "It can never make up for not having your love."

"I do love you."

She nodded, not entirely convinced. "Go upstairs to your wife," she said. "Better to fight it out than ignore poison."

He turned to the hall, but stopped dead. His father waited in the doorway, leaning against the jamb as if he couldn't stand without support. His eyes swam in tears, and Josh found himself choking again.

"How long have you been there?" he asked.

His dad didn't answer. Instead, he let go of the door and staggered toward Josh, who caught him. His dad's rough embrace was new and unfamiliar and yet vital.

Josh broke away, pretty sure he was going to cry if he didn't get out of there. "It's okay, Dad." His only thought was to reach his wife.

As if his need had traveled through the house's old timbers and reached her in their room, Lydia met him halfway down the stairs. "I shouldn't have run off like that," she said.

Below, the living room door closed on his parents.

"Let's go in here." He took her into the family room where someone had stoked the fire. He closed the doors, shutting his parents out, and Lydia sat on the love seat that had been reupholstered at least four times since his grandmother had owned it.

Continuity. His family had it. He'd rejected it, but it comforted Lydia, who'd been alone since she was eighteen.

"I want to tell you the truth," he said. "I don't want you to believe you can talk me into something different. We shouldn't waste time on false hopes or lies or games."

"I'm not playing games."

"Let me get this straight, please. I left my job in Hartford, but Kline is not our next stop."

"I know," she said, sad-eyed, "but let me ask one question. Where would we find this much land? We can make our home anything we want it to be. I'd design a workshop. You could rebuild one of those nineteen-thirties hot rods you've talked about. I'd love a small office of my own." She scooted aside to let him join her. A sound like bees departing fifty hives buzzed in his brain. "You love this land and so do I. Your grandfather gave it to you."

"I've just told you how I feel. I paid attention to what you wanted. Why can't you do me the same courtesy?" What part did such an antiseptic word have between a wife and husband?

"I'm sorry," she said. "I love being with family, and I believe you love your mother and father, too. If you hung in long enough around here, you'd get over your resentment. You'd stop wanting revenge."

"My sister died here. My parents let her die. I'm trying to make things right with my mother and father, but I can't change my real problem with this place. I couldn't save Clara. Do you think that memory fades?" Guilt almost stopped him as she ducked her head. "Any more than you'll forget losing our baby in Hartford?"

She looked up, her mouth trembling. "I'm sorry. I don't know why I wasn't thinking, except I've been caught up in creating some perfect future for us," she said. "You can't stay here for the same reason I don't want to go back."

"I've been trying to prove I'm not scared of what happened since Clara died. She depended on me, and I wasn't here. By the time I found her, she was gone."

"It wasn't your fault."

"I didn't say it was." Of course he had. A million times. He put the length of the room between them. Cold crept through the hundred-year-old window at his back, contrasting with heat from the fireplace.

"For better and worse, Josh. Till death does us part. I'm on your side, and I'm not going to leave you because your childhood still lives with you."

"You would have if I'd kept the job."

She nodded, slowly, surprised by her own resolve. "I think so. Because what's the point of a marriage if I'm afraid to have children with you? I want children, and I would never have tried again there. Do you know how many times we'd both have passed that courthouse where it happened?"

He grabbed the windowsill behind his back.

"Losing the baby reminds me how I felt when Clara died." His mother had reopened all the wounds. "It hurts, Lydia. Clara was so vulnerable. I can't help thinking I'm not good for children who depend on me."

Grief sharpened her face. Josh felt naked. Half an hour earlier, and he might have saved Clara. He hated thinking about it, but he rarely forgot.

Lydia stood, angry and certain and strong. "Our son never got a chance to depend on you because a stranger killed him." She came closer and held his face. "Clara was not your daughter. Were you supposed to quit school at fourteen so you could look after your little sister?"

The never-silent wind and sea whispered at him. He wanted everything he'd lost, his son and his sister. And his wife's happiness.

Lydia had held their baby boy inside her. She'd sworn she knew him from the way he moved. He hadn't liked pickles, and he'd kicked like crazy if she tried to sleep on her back. Josh had laughed at those tiny kicks against his palm.

Tears wet his eyes. He scrubbed them away. He'd been strong all his life—he'd taken chances to help people. He deserved a chance at happiness, and he wasn't a man who cried.

Lydia didn't seem to care if he cried. She put

her arms around him and pulled his head to her shoulder. "Give yourself a break, Josh. Lean on me and be sad until you can feel better."

He slid his arms around her, breathing deeply of her scent. But she leaned into him, and her breasts pillowed, soft against his chest. Her waist was narrower, her hipbones more prominent. She'd lost weight, but her body brought his a familiar, urgent ache.

They were weeks from making love, but he needed to lie in bed and hold her as close as she could come to him. "Let's go upstairs. I'm not upset." He smiled, echoing her earlier reassurance. "I just want to be your husband again."

"YOUR PARENTS are going to know we're in here."

Water beat down on them. Josh's arms held her tight. She blushed at the thought of Evelyn and Bart meeting them in the hall.

"I don't care." He said it against her ear. Warm water and Josh's arousal raised goose bumps from her head to her toes.

"This is leading us straight to frustration."

"Not as frustrating as lying beside you in that bed, never touching you." He lifted his head, staring at her mouth. "Now shut up and let's enjoy being together."

She stood on tiptoe before his mouth reached hers. At least the sound of the shower covered the crazy pounding of her heart. Josh trailed his fingertips down her back. She arched into him. Holding him was not going to be enough. She planted her palms on his shoulders and dragged her hands down his chest, pausing to bump over his nipples until he caught her wrists. She kissed him, taking in water and his breath and need.

Josh backed away. Only the shower wouldn't let him go far.

He smiled, lazily, sex in his gaze. "You were right." He pushed his wet hair off his forehead. "I'm feeling a little desperate—and frustrated."

"We should get out of here. Do you think they already know?"

"I don't care. We're adults."

They turned off the water and Lydia started to towel Josh off, but he stopped her. "Not a good idea," he said through gritted teeth.

She turned her back. He was suddenly behind her.

"Also not a good idea," he said, scooping her hair away from the side of her neck to kiss the sensitive skin.

She was getting nervous. "Let's go to our room, Josh."

"Sorry."

In a few minutes, she opened the door, checked to make sure his parents weren't in the hall and crept out, belting her robe at her waist. Josh followed in yet another pair of boxers.

The phone rang. His father picked it up from his and Evelyn's bedroom. "Geraldine? Hold on. It's for you, Evelyn."

Lydia opened Josh's bedroom door and hurried inside. He followed.

"I wonder what's going on," Josh said.

"These doors are like paper." Lydia wondered how well their voices had carried over running water. "Can you still hear your mom?"

"No." He looked at her, distracted, and she thought he was trying to hear if Geraldine's grandsons were in more trouble.

She was wrong. A second later, she was in his arms, and he took her mouth as if he hadn't really kissed her in years. A little bit of trust built a whole lot of longing. Holding him, touching, felt better each time.

When he released her, he didn't let her go. She clung to his shoulders, as unsteady as a brand-new bride. Joy lit his eyes with desire and triumph. He slid his hands down her arms, grinning as she shivered.

A knock at the door made them both jump. Lydia laughed nervously. Josh simply stared at her.

"I don't want to talk anymore," he said, low-voiced. "Just tell them I haven't killed you in case they thought we were arguing in the shower."

Lydia tightened her robe belt. "Hello?" she said, on some sort of lust-fuelled delay.

The door eased open, squeaking. Evelyn poked her head around it. She searched her son with a mother's concern. He moved behind Lydia, who couldn't help laughing again.

"I know it's late," Evelyn said, clearly aware she was intruding, "but we're running into town to see Geraldine. The Barkers made a counteroffer and we need to discuss my financing."

"Okay." Josh said. Lydia saw that something else was on his mind. Frustrated, he looked at his mom. "Anything else going on with Geraldine's grandsons?"

Lydia went still with shock. Josh had resisted any temptation to get involved in the problems of his hometown. His mother, equally surprised, made a quicker recovery.

"She wouldn't say." She started to leave. "She did tell me one thing. I asked because she sounded upset, but it's nothing the boys did."

"What, Mom?"

Evelyn glanced at Lydia, uncomfortable with spreading more gossip—which Lydia found endearing. "Their mother met a man, and she's asked Geraldine to let the boys stay on."

"Where's the father?" Josh asked.

"I don't know. Geraldine has no idea." She squared her shoulders. "Son, I know you're reluctant to work on a case while you're here, but this wouldn't be a real case."

Lydia felt his wary glance.

"What are you asking me?"

"Could you talk to those boys? Nobody likes the parking meters on the boardwalk anyway, but I've heard people are starting to keep Mitch and Luke out of their stores. They don't want to risk breakage or even theft. And that's going to affect Geraldine's business, too."

"You forget I'm the one who took Lydia to that pseudo-lineup. They might not like me because of that."

"They told their grandmother you didn't want to do it. They think they can't get into trouble because of the way you talked to Simon."

"That's a mistake. I was protecting Lydia."

"You need to act fast. They may think they have a free ride because someone like you believed in them. I don't know how much they know about our past."

"I never got in trouble. My goal was to get out of here."

"You chose to stay clean, despite having possibly the worst parents ever." Evelyn's face turned brick-red, but she stood tall, untouched by any other sign of shame. "Geraldine's grandsons didn't respond the same way when their parents abandoned them. They're the first kids everyone thinks of any time there's trouble now."

"I'm not staying here long enough to get in the middle of this, Mother."

"You help all those people who do horrible things. Why can't you try to persuade two boys to stop making bad choices before they need your services in court?"

Lydia wanted to agree, but this was happening in Kline, the one place Josh never wanted to stay a second longer than he had to. She'd already forced him to quit his job, but she'd try never to mention living here again.

"Geraldine might not want me guiding her boys. She may think I'm at the root of her problems because Lydia and I made the police talk to them about the school vandalism. She should talk to them."

Lydia turned to him. "Think how you'd respond to advice from your parents." She wished she hadn't said something so tactless in front of Evelyn, but she didn't try to apologize. "Sometimes an outsider is more convincing. I'm not pushing you, Josh, but your mom has a point about reaching them before they need a defense attorney."

"You aren't thinking I'll feel the need to stay here to stop two teenage boys from bugging the crap out of my old teacher?"

"I don't always have an ulterior motive." The answer came fast. "Surely you can trust me?"

His eyes reassured her with warmth left over from their shower. "But I'm not the best choice. Mom, those kids don't have real legal problems yet. They might be better off with someone who could talk to them about their parents."

"I'm going—I'll suggest that to Geraldine." Evelyn hugged Lydia and patted her son's arm. "I hoped I'd be able to offer Geraldine a few minutes of your time, but I understand." At the door, she paused without looking back. "As long as you're not holding out on helping them because you're still mad at your dad and me. If you are, I think you should get over it."

The door closed. Lydia, torn between the two of them, didn't know what to say.

"That killed the mood, huh?" Josh took her pajamas out of the closet and passed them to her. "You get the toothpaste first," he said.

"Aren't you even tempted?" she asked.

Ghosts looked out from his face, a boy who'd had his own share of problems, a young man who'd lost everything that had mattered, despite doing his best to hang on. "Old habits die hard," he said. "They remind me of myself, and I'd like to help them."

LYDIA TRIED to stay awake until Josh came to bed. The late hour and too many minutes packed into one day worked against her. She fell asleep, still waiting for the sound of his footsteps in the hall.

The next morning, she woke in the house alone. She washed up the coffee cups and her own breakfast dishes. After starting a load of laundry, she wandered out to the barn, hoping to find Josh and Bart.

They'd obviously skipped painting today in favor of paying work. She opened the barn and walked its length, exiting at least a football-field's distance later, into cold sunlight.

A woman who loved her share of cloudy days and wet weather, she still lifted her face to the benevolent warmth of a November sun. Behind her, a truck's engine roared. She turned. It was Bart's old truck, churning up dust on the gravel drive.

She started across the yard. Had Josh and his father had an accident on the boat? She saw only one man in the vehicle's cab. Josh got out at the kitchen doorway and waited for her.

"Morning," he said as she drew near enough to hear. "I hoped to see a little of you last night."

"Too much exercise. I fell asleep," she said with an attempt at a wry smile. "What's up?"

He hesitated, his eyes blank, his expression bland. "Come inside with me."

"Okay, but did something happen? Is Bart all right?"

"I ended up not going with him. I was with Mom, looking at secondhand ovens. Geraldine called and my conscience got the better of me." He held the mudroom door for her. "I'm not sure my mother didn't offer my services after all, but Geraldine asked me to talk to her grandsons, and…" He trailed off, obviously concerned about her reaction.

She went inside. "And what? Did she say something else?"

"No. It was—last night's lecture from my mother." He quirked an eyebrow. "And you."

A sense of relief surprised her. "I knew the

kinder, gentler Josh couldn't resist helping if he was still inside you."

"I'm not kinder or gentler. I just saw some sense in what you both said about redirecting these kids before they're in trouble."

"I'm teasing. Why'd you come home first?"

He looked down at the hole in his thermal shirt and the paint on his jeans. "I dressed to go with Dad before Mom asked me to look at ovens. You know how she's throwing her money around lately, and she doesn't even have the shop yet. Somehow I feel responsible for her."

"But you came home because Mitch and Luke care what you look like?"

"They probably won't talk to me anyway, but I thought I'd clean up to give a more…lucrative impression." He crossed the kitchen ahead of her. "Geraldine says the boys were picked up for drinking and driving last night. They're already at home—suspended from school for a fight that day Mom and I were talking to her. She suggested I could catch them before she sent them out to paint her garage."

"Must be the painting season in Kline," Lydia joked, anxious at the prospect of Josh dealing with another drinking problem.

"She got the idea from Dad and me."

In their room, he changed into newer jeans. She was leaning on the corner of his desk as he dropped his shirt on the floor. He stopped moving when he saw her looking at him. Josh covered the distance between them. He smiled as he lowered his head.

"You look as if you wouldn't mind…."

He was right. She took his clean sweater from his hands and pulled his arms around her, eager for his kiss. The sweater dropped on the floor in a heap as she slid her palms up his bare, tensed back. He felt so good. Holding him, she believed in one man above all others feeling right for a woman.

He eased away at last, but rubbed his thumb against the corner of her mouth. She bit him lightly, forgetting all the bad feelings that had torn them apart. Doubt and pain melted in the heated light of hope.

"It's not that I don't want to carry on," he said, "but your doctor ordered us not to."

"What does he know? He's just a man." She kissed him again, but he caught her hands, setting her away from him with flattering reluctance.

"I have to dress."

"Want some lunch before you go?"

"No." His tone reminded her of happier days, when they'd been more at ease, less likely to approach each other with caution. "Food is not on my mind right now."

She went downstairs and chose another book from his parents' shelves. She was sprawled on the sofa, not reading, when he came down.

"I forgot to ask how you're feeling," he said, smoothing his dark curls with his hands.

"Fine." She spread her arms, to show off her good health. "I'm on the mend in every way." She felt a spiral of sadness twist through her, but didn't share it with Josh. Sometimes, her grief for their child seemed like her own to deal with. "Did Geraldine mention how the bid's going?"

"I forgot to ask. When I agreed to talk to Mitch and Luke, I thought you might be upset."

She smiled, flawed enough to be happy.

"You don't have to look so pleased." Josh cradled her face to take the sting from his words.

"I'm smiling because I don't feel as if you're more interested in saving the world than being with me. In fact, I feel as if I got those boys in trouble in the first place, and I'm glad you're going."

"We're getting involved here, whether I want to or not." He thumbed her mouth again, his gaze locked on her lips. "But I'm begging you not to imagine I'll change my mind about staying."

"I won't." She could barely speak.

He nodded, but she knew he didn't believe her. She got up and stood on tiptoe to kiss him, looping one arm around his neck. "Persuade them to go straight, and you can wash your hands of Kline." She curved her mouth. "I'll try to want to as well."

He relaxed a little. "Want to go for a walk when I get back?"

"Sure."

"And track my mother if she calls." As his mouth drifted over her jaw, she inhaled. Josh held her with seductive tenderness.

Warnings clamored in Lydia's head. They'd talked, but they were still coasting. They'd agreed not to go home and not to stay here. But every time they tried to talk about the future, they came back to the past. Was she making the same old mistake?

"I'd better go." Josh skimmed her cheek with the back of his hand.

"Going is the right thing to do."

He gave her a crooked smile. She'd never sent him out to an unexpected meeting with a client with those words. He pushed through the door. She caught it before it slammed.

He strode to the car, his step ever more confident. The Josh she had loved had come back at last. Unable to resist attempting a good deed, he still made room for her in his priorities.

Would he stay this time? Or leave when he felt she was secure again? Wondering felt disloyal, but she couldn't just put the past few years out of her mind.

JOSH REACHED Geraldine's house with no memory of driving there. He rang the doorbell, with Lydia in his head, her body lithe and provocative, molding itself to his hands. He leaned against the door frame. Lost in wanting his wife, he hadn't considered what to say to these kids Geraldine had taken on.

The rowdier twin snatched the door open. Tall and skinny in the way of adolescents, he had the eyes of an old man.

"My grandmother's not here."

Josh had asked her not to tell the boys he was coming. They might have taken off.

"I'm looking for you." What would help him reach two kids who were nearly twenty years tougher than he'd been at their age? "And your brother."

"Too bad. You're not coming in. My grandmother says you and your wife might be helping the cops."

She could have altered that story before she'd asked him for help. Josh pushed his keys into his pockets. "I work as a defense attorney, but I was born in this town and I had some problems here. Your grandmother thought I might be able to talk to you."

"I need to see some ID."

Behind him, another kid, this one's carbon copy, showed up, worried as he eyed Josh. "Who is this guy, Mitch?"

"Do ya have to sound so scared?" the first kid asked with an ugly snarl. "Why don't you just admit we commit every crime in town? Thanks to this dude's wife, everyone thinks we do."

"Shut up. I told you I wouldn't testify against you." He shouldered Mitch out of the way. As he turned his face, Josh noticed the discoloration beneath his left eye. "I don't care how many cops or lawyers or women Chambers sends after us." He glanced back at his twin. The kid was losing his grip. "They aren't going to waste money prosecuting. You know what they said about court costs in Government class."

His injury and his naiveté tugged at Josh. He'd been that stupid once, but he'd never been stupid enough to blab in front of strangers when he should have kept his mouth shut. The first kid, Mitch, who'd probably hit his brother, obviously didn't appreciate protection from one of his victims. "I don't know what anyone said in some pointless class." He gave the boy who must be Luke a shove that bounced him into the doorjamb.

It was all too damn familiar. He'd seen it dozens of times. Luke and Mitch were trying to brazen it out. Mitch, bullying his less belligerent brother into line.

"Luke, as I told your brother, I'm an attorney," Josh said. "My mother is your grandmother's client. My name is Josh Quincy. Do you two need representation?"

"Shut up, Luke," Mitch said before his brother could utter another reckless word.

As if they'd planned it, both boys planted their hands on their hips.

"Fine." Josh had fulfilled his promise to their grandmother. He felt no compunction about leaving another puffed-up drunk, no matter what his age, to sort out his own problems. "I'm wasting my time."

"Wait."

That would be Luke.

Josh turned back. Mitch rammed an elbow into Luke's ribs. Luke hardly flinched, which troubled Josh a lot more than anything they'd said.

"What else have you been up to, Mitch?" he asked with a quick glance at the other boy.

The thug just laughed. Josh understood being last on a parents' list, wondering why you weren't good enough for love. But he couldn't find empathy for a kid who beat up his brother to get back at his mother and father.

"Look, my mom offered your grandmother a favor. I had some problems and I ended up in a foster home, milking cows for my supper."

"So you're going to talk some sense into us," Mitch said, all mockery. His hand was white where he gripped his brother's arm.

"I don't see how I could." The kid knew nothing and wanted to know less. Maybe a little punishment would be just the anvil he needed on his thick skull. Too bad about the fine Geraldine would have to pay on this brat's behalf, but the commission she was about to receive from his mother's business would no doubt arrange her finances.

At his car, Josh looked back, concentrating on Luke. "Give me a call if you need anything. I'm at Bart and Evelyn Quincy's."

Mitch shoved his brother back inside and slammed the door. Josh swore, climbing back into the car. Couldn't he just stop?

Indeed he could not. He called his mother so she could report his lack of progress to Luke and Mitch Dawson's grandmother.

CHAPTER TWELVE

TWELVE DAYS LATER, JOSH'S mother took possession of Barker's Café. The Barkers had been as eager as she to tie things up.

Happily, Lydia had been too cautious to hope Josh's visit with the Dawson boys would change his attitude toward his hometown. He'd said nothing except that his mother and the boys' grandmother had been wrong. Mitch and Luke hadn't needed him.

He and Lydia spent their evenings searching the Internet from Josh's laptop for real estate listings. Josh had actually suggested Boston, but he'd given up so quickly in the face of her dismay that she doubted his seriousness.

Thus far, they couldn't agree on a town. Their truce had grown semitouchy as they both found reasons to knock one location after another off their list.

On the morning his mom started moving her

things into the café, Josh drove his parents to their attorney's office to seal the real estate deal. Lydia shopped for provisions for a surprise meal of lobster and corn and potatoes. She added fresh garlic bread and a crisp salad of field greens and greenhouse tomatoes to her New England celebration.

Josh and his parents were already home when she got back. She carried the groceries past Evelyn's SUV and climbed the steps to the porch. Evelyn met her in the mudroom, her arms laden with a mop and broom and a box of cleaning supplies.

"What are you doing?" Lydia asked.

"I can't wait. It's all mine and I'm going to make it shine. The sooner I open, the better I'll like it."

"Bart was going to hire someone." Lydia grimaced, remembering too late that Bart had planned to surprise his wife.

"What?" The idea offended Evelyn's natural austerity. "Why would we waste that kind of money?" She eased around Lydia's armload. "Do you want to come? Josh and Bart are helping." She stopped, shaking her head. "No. No. You shouldn't overdo it."

"I'm fine." It was true. Her body felt stronger each day. In a terrible irony, healing made her strangely sad because it seemed to distance her from her baby. On the other hand, with more energy, she began to hear life calling. "I'd love to help out. Where are the guys?"

"Bart must be upstairs calling off his cleaners. Josh went up to change." Evelyn tiptoed to peer at Lydia's bags. "What all did you buy?"

"Lobster and corn and stuff." She set it on the counter, but then took the lobster out and maneuvered it into the full fridge.

"I appreciate the thought, honey, but we'll be too tired to cook tonight. Why don't we drop off the lobster for Geraldine?"

"Are you sure? I thought you'd want to celebrate."

"She worked so hard for me," Evelyn said. "And she could use some luxury."

"Sounds good." Lydia lowered her voice. "I'd like to see Mitch and Luke eye to eye without Simon Chambers pressuring me to identify them."

Evelyn glanced up at the sounds of Josh walking overhead. "Geraldine hasn't said a word about them except to thank Josh for trying. I don't know what's going on. He didn't seem too pleased with the results."

"That's why I haven't had the courage to ask him anything else. He was disappointed, but he also seemed a little annoyed."

He came down the stairs, pulling a sweatshirt over his head. "What are you two whispering about?"

"Geraldine's boys," his mother said. "Have you heard anything from them?"

"I don't expect to. Mitch is too angry to care about advice, good or bad, and Luke won't go against his brother."

"Go against him?" Lydia moved close to Josh, where she liked to be these days. "What do you mean?"

"I don't know the specifics." He looked at his mother. "Has Geraldine told you anything she didn't mention to me?"

Evelyn shook her head.

Josh went on, "I'd bet Mitch keeps his brother in line with physical force. Geraldine either knows, or she refuses to see."

"He's hurting him?" Lydia, too familiar with violence, made Josh face her. "We have to do something."

"I tried to give Luke an opening to tell me what his brother's done. He refused."

"We have to make him talk."

"Who are you all of a sudden?" he asked.

"A changed woman and, whether you like it or not, part of this town for now. If Mitch is hitting

Luke, he'll move on to someone else. And Luke needs protection."

"Wait, both of you," Evelyn said. "Did you ever wonder why Children's Services never came to take Josh and Clara away from us?"

"Mother—"

"Yes," Lydia said. "Why?"

"Because Josh hid the truth, and Clara, being home most of the time, had no opportunity to let the truth slip."

"I know children protect their abusers," Lydia said, "but responsible adults step in when children need help."

"I tried to step in," Josh said, "but I can't force Luke to let me help him, and Mitch would rather set the world on fire than be safe."

"Are you talking about the school?"

"I'm certainly more willing to understand why Simon considers him a suspect. How much anger does it take to make a guy clock his twin brother?"

"What are you going to do?" Lydia asked. "I'll come with you. I'll flat out tell Luke he has to come clean about his brother."

"You won't go anywhere near them." Josh's voice pierced their uneasy peace. "I mean it." He took her face in both hands. She felt the pulse in his wrist. "If Mitch touched you, I'd kill him. Seriously, Lydia. Kill him. You don't want that."

"Somehow I trust you more than you trust yourself. You know at least one of those boys needs help."

"I'm warning you." He took a deep breath, but he couldn't seem to speak for a moment. "Or I'm begging you—don't get any more involved with the Dawson kids."

"I can't stand by while some bully beats his brother, because I'm afraid. Violence makes me furious."

Lydia caught sight of Evelyn, appalled, with tears making her eyes liquid. Somehow they'd become a family. She was responsible to the people in this house, too—no longer detached.

"Josh, we both knew we had to change when we came here. I won't let that hoodlum scare me." She closed her hands around his and eased his right palm to her lips. He shuddered at her kiss, leaving her uncertain. She let him go. "I won't do anything," she said. "But I can't stand thinking Mitch is hurting his own brother. Can't we talk to Simon?"

"That won't do any good." Josh gathered himself, avoiding his mother's watery gaze. "They've already been arrested once for drinking.

They're out on bail. Don't tell Geraldine I told you, Mom, but the system Simon's so proud of will force Luke and Mitch to tell who did what."

"I should make Geraldine talk about this." Evelyn sounded miserable. "What good is a friend you don't trust?"

"If she didn't tell you the truth about the boys, she thinks you don't know. Don't force sympathy on her. How would you take that from her?"

She hitched her cleaning supplies tighter. "You're pretty smart, considering the amount of help you had from your father and me." She pointed toward the fridge. "Josh, Lydia put some lobster in there. Take it out. We're going to give it to Geraldine and give her a chance to talk at the same time. She may not realize she's safe with us. How she can think I'd judge her…"

Josh pulled the lobster out. "We don't have to beat the dead past anymore. Let's just let it lie and see where we go from here."

Lydia took a step toward him. They'd handled their own problems the same way—never discussing them. And they weren't safe yet. But he turned, his eyes tired, his mouth strained and thin. She couldn't suggest yet again that he was making a mistake. He needed empathy.

"I'll go with you to Geraldine's." She offered

the bag she'd brought the meal's ingredients home in. "Put the box in here."

"No." He stored the container in the bag. "You go nowhere near that family. I know you don't like me thinking I know best, but I couldn't help you with Vivian, and I do feel guilty. Please don't let that kid close enough to hurt you."

"What about you?" He wasn't impervious. "Do you really think Mitch is dangerous?"

He considered. At least he didn't try to put her off. "He is to Luke—his own twin—that's enough evidence for me."

"You're so worried about what these boys will do, you're scaring me, too. I don't want you hurt."

"I'll be fine with clients who'll never need to know you exist, but these kids know you and my mother and father. I'm not sure what's going on with Mitch, but I get a bad feeling from him."

"I'm coming with you. Don't even consider arguing."

"Thanks, Lydia." His dry grin stopped her in mid-rant. Laughter, when she was trying to make him see sense might annoy her, but she could bathe in his affection. "I don't know how to put this without being offensive, but what would you do if I was in trouble?"

She thought. "The same thing you'd do for me. Anything."

"Oh." He cleared his throat. "Okay. We'll drop off the lobster. Then we'll meet you at Barker's."

"At Grandma Trudy's." Evelyn made no attempt to hide her pride, but her smile didn't make it all the way to her mouth.

"Grandma Trudy's. You two are driving me nuts."

Lydia wanted to laugh for joy. She and her husband might be on a seesaw, but she was proud of him for the headway he'd made with his parents.

"What can be keeping your father?" Evelyn finished carrying her things out to the car and then honked. Bart thundered down the stairs and then ran through the kitchen, muttering a goodbye. "Gotta get the drill out of the tool shed. And a sander. That woman."

Lydia buttoned her coat at the throat. "How do they stay so close?"

"It's that or start drinking again."

"What do you mean?"

Josh turned to the other shopping bags. "Mom said they got sober and talked their problems out. They could hardly split up with me to come home to. I didn't realize it at the time, but they were responsible enough to try to make up to me for what happened to Clara. So they had to stick together. Imagine facing a reminder of that guilt every day."

"Did you see them often in prison?"

"Never." He looked inside the rest of the shopping bags. "I didn't want to, and my foster parents had better things for me to do." He eyed the milk jug as he took it from a bag. "Cows. Thousands of cows."

"Thousands, huh?" As always, she burned at the idea of supposed caregivers forcing Josh to work so hard as a kid.

"I went from udder to udder, with a break in between to thaw out my fingers."

"That bugs me every time I hear it."

"Does it?" He stored another gallon of milk in the fridge. "I always wondered if every foster home required indentured servitude."

"We should find out if it's changed."

Josh nodded at the other bags. "That's everything that needs cold storage. Let's go."

"You don't think Mitch would hurt Geraldine?"

"I looked at her pretty carefully this morning. She wore long sleeves, but winter is here. She didn't seem to move as if anything hurt." He picked up the lobster dinner bag and reached for the door ahead of her. "Speaking of which, you move as if you're feeling better."

Knowing he was watching her, she felt stiff. "I am." Cold air blew in as he opened the mud-room door. "Do you think we'll still be here for Thanksgiving?"

"That's up to you. If you want to move we have to go back to Hartford and pack up the town house." He looked down at her, and he seemed taller. Or maybe more remote. "We have to agree on some place."

"I know. Maybe we've been searching the wrong way. You should call around and see which towns have openings for a public defender." She tried to open the car door, but it was locked.

"I've considered opening my own office." He fumbled with the keys and punched the keyless entry. "I still wouldn't make a fortune, because I'm not changing the type of client I've been defending, but maybe I'm tired of the Brice Deans of the world."

"Brice had more of a clear-the-case mentality," she said.

"You were listening when I complained."

She shrugged. "I thought Brice should do more for his employees' security."

Josh didn't answer. As time crept by, and she learned she'd have to live with loss that didn't seem to lessen, Lydia realized neither Josh nor his boss could have stopped Vivian Durance. She'd decided Lydia should pay for her husband's capital sentence.

It was a quiet drive to Geraldine's. Josh parked and grabbed the shopping bag. "I'll take it up."

"We settled this. I'm going, too."

"They're not average kids, Lydia."

"I'd like to say hello to Geraldine."

"Uh-huh." He opened his door. "With you guarding my back, I know no fear."

Let him make fun. She marched up Geraldine's steps at his side. At the top, standing in front of the small blue-painted box of a house, he took her hand.

Lydia knocked on the white door. She smiled absently at Josh as she glanced past him. This narrow street ended at the high school.

"They don't live far from—"

Geraldine opened up. "Josh." She widened her eyes at Lydia. It appeared neither guest was welcome. The boys must have been angry after their last visit. "What's going on? Didn't your mother's keys work?"

Josh held up the lobster. "They worked fine, but she wanted us to drop these off as a thank-you."

Geraldine took the sack and opened it. Everyone in town recognized Lender's Seafood packaging. "Does your father know you bought lobster from a rival?"

"Evelyn decided what to give you on the spur of the moment." Lydia's skin warmed as she lied.

"How lovely, but she didn't have to do that. I got a nice commission."

"I think it's more a thank-you because you supported her in buying Barker's when I thought she should consider the other places," Josh said.

"Also my job." Geraldine twisted the bag closed. "Thanks again. I'll call her later tonight. Lydia, you have much better color."

"I'm improved, thank you. How are your grandsons?"

Josh's fingers clenched hers, but the boys were their real reason for coming, and clearly things weren't going well with them. Geraldine looked everywhere but at Lydia.

"Luke and Mitch are great. Just fine."

One of the boys staggered down the stairs behind her, his hair oily, his dark khaki shirt big enough to accommodate his twin as well. He eyed Lydia with hostility. Then he saw Josh and scowled as if the juvenile authorities had shown up.

"Whaddaya want?"

"A word with your grandmother. This is Mitch, Lydia." Josh's sarcasm wasn't lost on her. Mitch probably hadn't missed it either. "I'd recognize him anywhere."

"It's nice to see you under better circumstances," she offered.

Mitch glowered at her. "Yeah?"

She felt sick.

Geraldine sprang into action. "Thanks so much for the lobster. Tell your mother we'll enjoy it, but I think we'll have to wait for tomorrow night."

"I'm not helping at your booth tonight," Mitch said. "I have a date for that fish fry."

"Shrimp boil." Geraldine smiled, but a hint of anxiety leaked through. "The Rotary Club is holding a shrimp boil at the armory. Maybe you all planned to go?"

"My mother's enlisted us to clean the shop," Josh said. "I'm not sure when we'll finish." Something in his tone alerted Lydia as his glance brushed Mitch.

She sensed they'd be looking for the troubled boy later.

"We'll probably be there until late," Geraldine said.

"Gran." Mitch was clearly trying to shut his grandmother up.

She only smiled. "Luke already left. Did you walk from the shop?" Then she saw the car. "Oh. I thought you might have seen him along the way."

"Gran." Mitch came to the door. "I don't know what you think this guy can do for us, but Luke and I don't want him." He turned to Josh. "So leave us alone."

It'd take more than one angry kid to put Josh off. "Stop by the store, Mitch." He lowered his voice. Lydia had rarely visited his office or watched him in court after she'd stopped feeling safe. She'd forgotten how subtly he defused a situation. "Mother packed cookies in case anyone dropped by."

His refusal to get angry worked the opposite effect on Mitch. The boy turned on him, almost out of control. "Why don't you get the fu—"

Geraldine slammed the door before he could finish. Lydia stared at the painted panels, an unwilling witness.

"He could hurt her."

"I don't think he will." Josh nodded at her doubt. "He was different with Luke. He was obviously in charge. He's still struggling with Geraldine for power."

Lydia decided on bluntness. "We've proven we're the worst at assessing actual intimidation."

Josh pulled her down the steps. "I see your point. Why don't I look for him later and maybe have a word with him about Geraldine?"

"And Luke." She touched her stomach. "I don't care if I'm overreacting. One day he'll grow up, and surely regret hurting his own family."

Josh opened the car door for her again. "When I was Mitch's age, I'd have given a lot for someone like Geraldine."

"I'd like a few minutes alone with his parents. We nearly split up because we lost our son, and they've abandoned their boys."

Josh's set expression made Lydia realize how much the Dawsons' situation was reminding him of his own childhood.

"I'm sorry I got you into this," she said when he took the steering wheel, "but I wonder if we should make sure Geraldine knows what Mitch is doing to Luke."

"Good idea, but what if she does know? She loves both boys, and she might lie to protect him."

"Surely she couldn't choose one at the risk of harm to the other?"

"I don't know." He started the car. "She told me about the DUI, but she didn't tell me everything. If she knows, she's ashamed or deliberately closing her eyes." He looked at Lydia as he put the car in gear. "Which we know to be a mistake."

He had changed. He was taking Mitch's threats seriously.

"EVELYN, what would you think of knocking down this wall and giving your customers a view of the kitchen?" Lydia seemed engrossed in structural changes.

"What? Knock down the wall?" His mother fluttered with alarm as if Lydia had suggested maiming a dear friend.

Josh leaned his mop against the wall and eased outside, holding the bell so that it barely tinkled. Wind grabbed at his hair and sprayed ocean water at his face.

Grandma Trudy would be lucky if someone looked up from the sidewalk on an evening like this. Moving beyond the shop's windows, he dialed Geraldine's number, but got her answering machine. "Just calling to say thanks again from my mother—" He checked the anger he found hard to control. "—since we left so abruptly. I hope you and the boys enjoy the lobster."

Lydia's anxiety for Geraldine was contagious. The explanation for her unanswered phone might be simple. She could be out with another client, or she might have left for the armory already.

Sand scudded along the almost empty boardwalk. He lowered his head to blink a handful out of his eyes. It'd take a stern customer to shop for property in weather like this.

He returned to the store. Lydia had joined his dad in repainting the white walls.

"Lydia, what the hell?"

She and his father turned and then froze, their long-handled rollers raised.

"It hasn't even been four weeks. You shouldn't be painting."

"I'm fine." Color flooded her face. "Look at everything I've done since we came here. Besides, I like to paint." As if she realized she was holding the roller in a parody of the Statue of Liberty, she lowered it and his father followed. "Thanks for asking, though."

"Maybe I was abrupt." She nodded. He took the roller. She could listen to him for once. "But, Dad, you know Lydia's not supposed to overexert."

"Blame your mother," Bart said. "She was almost hysterical at the thought of touching a nail in this building. She scared Lydia."

Josh leaned over to dip the drying roller in paint. "I can see that, but take shelter with a book—in a chair, Lydia."

"I'm not an invalid. I'm better and you're embarrassing me."

"In front of my dad?"

"If she's all right to chase after troubled teens, she's fine to paint. Give the woman a break."

Josh looked up, willing to accept a challenge, even from his father.

"Back off," Lydia said. "We're all on the same side, and if you two don't lower the tension, I'll go suggest your mother add enclosed booths in here."

"I can't afford that." Bart waved his son toward the wall. "Step up. If we finish this, we get shrimp."

That suited Josh. A discreet new look at Mitch and Luke and the friends they hung out with would tell him plenty.

"WE'VE BEEN UP and down this place three times." Lydia patted her stomach. "I'm so full of shrimp it's starting to spill out my ears, but I'm starting to think Mitch kept Luke away once he thought we might show up."

Josh linked his fingers with hers. "After I complained to you and Dad, I'm wearing you out. Why don't you sit and I'll make one more circuit. If I don't find them, we'll go."

"I'll lean on a spot near the door." She took a conspiratorial tone. "They won't get past me."

Laughing, he pulled her close and kissed her temple. He walked away smiling, and Lydia enjoyed her view of him in jeans and a sweater that emphasized the breadth of his shoulders. How long since she'd looked at him and thought, "That man is my husband. I'm a lucky woman"?

She cracked a small smile at the grizzled fisherman, who was holding up the wall nearest the door. He'd clearly come to the community shrimp boil straight from his boat. His aroma could put a woman off.

He held up his plate. "Starving," he said.

She nodded.

"You're Bart Quincy's daughter-in-law."

"I forget what a small place Kline is."

"Yeah—everybody knows everybody. We're all surprised Josh is back here. This town was always too small for him."

"No." She defended him without thinking. "He just never has much time off from work." She leveled a look at the other man's salt-stained, fishy overalls. "You know how that is."

"Yes, ma'am."

They reached an amicable silence.

It turned out that waiting at the door was the best way to find the Dawsons. Pushing his brother ahead of him, Mitch parted Luke from the crowded floor. Lydia tried to make herself small. Luke saw her. He dropped his head and then stopped, coming to a decision. He faced his brother, bracing both hands on the door.

"I'm not going, man. I've had it. You want it— you go. I'm staying here."

"Chicken." Mitch made the classic clucking sound, but Luke only waved a disgusted hand at his brother and stomped away. Mitch caught up with Luke, leaning over to say something that was plainly a threat.

Whatever he'd said made Luke stare at his brother and then shove him in anger. Laughing, Mitch leered at Lydia before he continued his exit from the armory.

Luke gave her one last wary glance and then sank back into the crowds. She hated his fear. She wrapped her arms around her waist. No child should feel like that, no matter how old he was.

Lydia straightened, looking for Josh, but seeing no sign of him. Mitch had to be up to trouble. She couldn't let him go. He might hurt someone else. She wanted to loathe him, with the kind of rage she'd felt toward Vivian Durance, but he was just a kid, an angry kid, whose family had let him down.

He reminded her of Josh, and he might do something in this mood that would change his life forever.

She had to go after him.

"Excuse me," she said to her fisherman friend and darted around him, through the door. Down the sidewalk, buffeted by wind and sea and rain, Mitch was hurrying alongside the empty shop fronts.

Lydia held back. He probably couldn't hear her in this weather, but she gave him time to get ahead of her.

Fighting the storm and sand and cold that drilled straight to her bones, Lydia found she'd given him too large a lead. She lost him. When she looked up from a strong buffet of rain, he'd gone. Simply disappeared.

She looked back at the armory, at the far end of the boardwalk. No light, other than the dim ones left by their owners, shone from any building. Mitch must have ducked down one of the narrow alleys.

She turned back, staring down the darkened streets, waiting for movement, since she could hardly see. Tucked into the corner of a photo shop, she stood stock-still when Mitch swung out of an alley.

Holding something—a box—in his hands, he peered just as Lydia had. He didn't want to be seen. She relaxed as far as she could into darkness.

He emptied the box into his hand. Something clinked, even through the howling wind. He dropped the box and ground it into the sidewalk. Then he strode off as if bright sunlight and calm seas beckoned.

Lydia waited for him to go back inside the

armory. Her heart pounded as she ran for the box.
His shoe had all but glued it to the wet sidewalk,
but she read the blurred print. Bullets. .22 caliber.

She ran.

CHAPTER THIRTEEN

JOSH'S PHONE RANG. He opened it, and someone was speaking, but he couldn't discern words over the crowd noise.

"Lydia? Is that you?"

"Who else? I've called you three times. Where are you?"

"In the armory. I guess I didn't hear my phone." Wind was roaring from hers. "Where are you?" He started for the front doors.

A family turned in unison ahead of him and he saw his wife. He shut his phone and went to her. She wasn't hurt, but he took inventory to make sure.

"Let me go. We have to find Mitch."

"Why so urgent?"

"Look at this."

He took the tattered, wet cardboard. "Bullets? Where did you get it?"

"Mitch broke into a store down one of those

alleys toward your mom's place, and then he emptied the bullets into his hand and dropped this. If he took these, he must have a gun. We have to tell Geraldine."

Josh shook his head. "I like Geraldine, but she's not doing them any good. I'm calling Simon."

Lydia caught his arms. Her eyes were almost too bright. "I care so much about this kid because he makes me think of you."

He tried to shake her off. "I was never like that boy. I had real problems, and I never hurt anyone if I could help it."

"Because you made good choices." She grabbed his arms again. His wife possessed more strength than he'd realized. "If someone had helped your family, maybe no one would have gone to jail. You might not have lost your sister. Give Geraldine a chance, but if she can't do what she has to, we'll call Simon."

"I understand this situation better than you do, Lydia. He could hurt you."

"I know that."

Tempted to argue, he made himself stop. He headed for the quietest corner he could find. Lydia stuck like glue. Geraldine answered on the first ring.

"I have to tell you something about Mitch." He

related Lydia's story. "We think he has a gun if he's stealing bullets."

Geraldine was silent. For a moment. He turned toward the huge room, searching for either of her grandsons.

"Luke?" he said in a whisper to Lydia.

Shrugging, she pointed to the citizens of Kline, crammed into the building.

"Mitch doesn't have a gun." Geraldine's voice sank to a whisper. She cleared her throat. "I'll go home and search his room before he gets there." Her dread traveled all the way through the phone.

He didn't blame her. What grandparent wanted to go through her grandson's personal things, expecting a lethal weapon? "Searching isn't enough. You have to tell Simon Chambers."

"I will. I don't want anything to happen to Mitch."

"Or to Luke and you. I think he gave Luke that black eye."

"I'll take care of this, Josh. Thanks for your help." She shut him out with a New Englander's repressiveness.

"I'll have to tell Simon if you don't. Mitch is angry with my wife, and I won't leave her in danger. That kid will be better off if he explains what he's doing and why."

Geraldine thanked him again and hung up. Josh shut his phone and faced Lydia, who was lost in thought. "Why aren't you afraid?"

"I've been wondering that same thing." She laid her hand across his forearm. "I think it's because we're together. Really together, for the first time in years."

She broke his heart. It was that simple—because she'd doubted him, and now she didn't. "I was always on your side," he said.

"I couldn't tell." He pulled her as close as she could get, close enough that he seemed to feel her heart beating. "I'm not confused now," she said. "I know I matter most to you. Neither of us knew how to work at marriage before."

He kissed the top of her head, then glanced back at his phone.

He dialed Geraldine again. She answered, but her breath rattled. "I'm busy, Josh. What do you want?"

"Has he come home?"

"No. I'm still searching his room."

"Have you called Simon?"

"Not yet." She stopped whatever she was doing to sound defensive. "I will."

"I can't wait for you to do that. I have to because of Lydia."

"Josh, please."

"I'm sorry, Geraldine. I have to protect my family, too. I am sorry."

He hung up and then called the police station. A dispatcher connected him with Simon.

"What can I do for you, Josh?"

"Hold on." He passed the phone to Lydia and she told her story about chasing Mitch in the dark. The more he thought about that, the angrier he grew. They seemed to have switched sides on the safety argument.

"What?" She craned her neck to look around the room. "I see a patrolman by the punch bowl." Startling Josh, she laughed. "Sorry—I didn't mean to get him in trouble. Consider it community policing."

Josh made an impatient move, and she got back on track. "We'll go to him, but I haven't seen Mitch or Luke since I came back."

The patrolman's phone rang immediately after Lydia hung up. He was getting off the line by the time they reached him. He shook Lydia's hand.

"You're supposed to stay with me until the chief gets here."

"Right," she said.

"Do you know Mitch and Luke?" Josh asked, moving so that Lydia was somewhat sheltered between him and the cop.

"Unfortunately." The younger man scanned the crowds. "They've been headed down this road for about a year. Too bad, too, because I remember when they came by the station as part of some school program to wash the patrol cars, not to soap them."

"Alcohol and a gun up the ante," Josh said.

"I'm surprised at you saying that."

"Me, too." Josh put one arm around his wife. She'd changed him. He looked at her anxious face. He'd changed her, too.

Finally, Simon arrived and took notes as Lydia repeated her story. There was still no sign of the teenagers.

"And you maintain you don't know if they were the boys who tried to break into the school?"

She shrugged. "I just don't know."

He flipped his notebook shut. "Okay. You should go home." He glanced at Josh. "You both know that Mitch and Luke are angry with Lydia. Lie low till we find him—and his gun. I think I'll send a patrol car by tonight."

"Thanks," Josh said.

Then he called his parents, also lost in the crowd, and filled them in. Knowing he was over-reacting, he tried to protect Lydia with his body as he walked her to their SUV and headed to the home that had never meant safety to him before. A patrol car passed as he turned into the driveway.

He headed slowly toward the house, searching the headland and the yard for any sign of an angry kid. It was like looking for himself, only he'd hidden out there to escape his parents.

"It looks all right. Let's go."

Lydia clung to his hand. He hurried her, but tried not to run. "You're more worried than I am," she said.

"Because I've seen the worst people can do." He closed his mouth, swearing silently. How much worse did Lydia ever need to see? "Sorry," he said.

"Don't. I'm learning to abide. I miss him, and I wonder who he would have been, what he would have looked like. Maybe he'll always be an ache in my heart."

"And mine."

"I don't forget that."

"You've both made me too aware," Josh said, slightly vexed.

Smiling faintly as if she wasn't quite on his plane, she turned toward the stairs. "I'm tired, think I'll brush my teeth."

He watched her go up, wishing he hadn't reminded her tonight. Sometimes he suspected she went to bed first to avoid him.

Two steps forward—twenty back. Work at marriage? It was a frustrating, full-time job.

But he was tired of failing.

JOSH WAS WAITING in their room when she entered after her shower. "I thought you were only brushing your teeth," he said.

"Busy day. And we worked a lot." He seemed remote, sprawled in his old desk chair, his feet in front of him, his expression brooding and impossible to read. "Brush yours, too," she said.

He frowned in a wordless question.

She laughed and nearly choked, her throat was so dry. Fear did that to a woman, and she was afraid of the chance she was about to take. "I want you to stay with me, and I didn't know how to ask. I thought tooth brushing would be a subtle hint."

He remained motionless. "I don't understand you."

"Because, just like you, I tend to put my pride first, and I don't want to be the one who cares more."

"You don't," he said.

"Care more?" she asked. He nodded. "Every night, we share this bed. You put your arm around me. You kiss me good night, but we haven't talked about where we're going. We're waiting again for the decision to make itself."

"As long as we go together, it doesn't matter," he said. Then he stood. "That's not true, is it? Every time we've discussed a new town, one of us finds a reason not to move there." He grabbed a pair of boxers and a clean towel. "Don't go to sleep," he said at the door.

Again, heat flooded her cheeks. "Hurry. Your mother and father will want to talk about Mitch, and we can't do anything about it tonight."

The water barely came on before it went off again. Lydia dropped her robe on the desk chair and climbed into bed, yanking her short gown down her thighs.

She didn't even pretend to read.

Josh came back, wearing only boxers and damp hair. He shut their door and turned off the light and then crossed to open the blinds on the window. Lightning flickered through the room.

"What are you thinking, Lydia? It hasn't been six weeks."

Lydia was glad he couldn't see her blushing even harder. "I just want to lie in your arms, the way I used to."

He pressed a kiss to her hair. She moved and caught his mouth. She welcomed his touch, sighed when he cupped her breast. But he stilled his restless, teasing hand and then spoke against her forehead. "Have mercy."

"I want you, too." She ached for him, longed to feel him inside her, breathing only in tandem, as the one being they had promised to become so long ago. She slid her own hand down his flat belly, loving his silky hair against her fingers.

"You're killing me."

She laughed, finding pleasure in his hoarseness. "I'm the one who can't..." She kissed his chest, following the rise and fall of his uneven breathing. "For you, I could—"

"I don't want that." He turned down her unspoken offer. He laughed. "Well—I want it, but when we both can is time enough."

Safe in the tight-buttoned house on the edge of the sea, Lydia longed to admit she loved him and always would, no matter what job he took, or where he needed her to go.

Her own insecurity demanded too much. His actions, choosing her, holding her, needing her in all the ways a husband could, had chased danger from her mind. It was enough to sleep on.

"Put your arms around me," Josh said, "but try not to rub—anywhere."

Laughing, she wrapped herself around him. Gingerly.

STORMS HUNG over them for the following week. The weather was too dangerous for fishing and not fit for painting the barn. With no word on either of the Dawson twins, Evelyn put them all to work in the shop.

On Friday, she delegated cookie wrapping to Lydia, ingredient measuring to Bart and cleaning out the walk-in freezer to Josh. Lydia bristled at having such a small task.

"You have to be precise though," Evelyn said. "Or they'll come undone and dry out. We don't want that."

Rankled, Lydia took a refilled coffee mug, printed with Grandma Trudy's label to the freezer for Josh.

"Thanks." He gripped it in his gloved hands. "I'm freezing."

"We should have taken all this stuff home," Lydia said. Evelyn had already started filling the freezer so he couldn't unplug it to clean.

"Now you think of it." He grinned. "How's Dad?"

"Swearing at flour, last time I saw him."

The door, which Lydia had left cracked, opened all the way. Evelyn leaned in. "Josh, Geraldine's here. She'd like to talk to you."

"Is she all right?" He went, shucking off clothing.

"Upset." Evelyn leaned closer. "But I didn't see bruises."

Lydia took Josh's coat and scarf and gloves. In the café, he met Geraldine with an outstretched hand. She didn't bother to shake it, falling into his arms instead. If the woman hadn't been on the verge of crying, Lydia might have laughed at her husband's look of bewilderment.

"Mitch?" he asked, his expression already distracted as he began to formulate the boy's next step.

"No. It's Luke. He came back last night, but he didn't tell me he had a court date today for the DUI. He took the letter out of the mail and hid it. Only he wasn't drinking or driving. It was Mitch, and he forced Luke to hand over his ID. Please come help him, Josh."

"I'm not licensed to practice in Maine."

"Tell him what to do then."

"He should ask for a continuance."

"Why? He did nothing except give in to his brother. Please, Josh."

He turned to Lydia, who hated the idea of him in court, but realized her reaction was visceral and had nothing to do with reality. "You should go," she said.

"Where's Mitch?"

"He came home this morning. I guess he couldn't last without his brother, no matter how tough he claims to be. I asked him about the bullets. He said he found them, but he has no gun."

"He's lying to you. Take him to Simon Chambers and make him give it up. What time is Luke due in court?"

"Two o'clock."

"I'll pick him up." He took his things from Lydia. "You don't need to stay here any longer. Come home with me."

"I'm fine."

He tugged her closer, as if he could hide what he was saying from his mother and father. "I don't want to leave you here. I'm not being rational, but come home. Please."

"All right." She felt too much empathy for Geraldine to delay Josh with an argument. "Let me get my coat. I'll start dinner, Evelyn."

"Thanks, honey. Although we may not stay much longer ourselves." This, she said to Josh, probably to reassure him that Lydia wouldn't be home alone long. "I can't take your father's grousing, and goodness knows how his bad attitude will affect my cooking."

Josh drove fast and silently, his mind no doubt on Luke Dawson's problems. At the house, he hustled her inside again. Lydia let him get away with overprotecting her because his mind was elsewhere.

"Why are you so intent on Mitch going to the police?" she asked.

"He's out of control, and Geraldine won't take care of the problem. If he doesn't have a parent figure, the police will have to step in, but fooling around with a gun is too serious for an eighteen-year-old boy."

"Man, technically."

"I know." He locked the door. "All the more reason to handle it." He pulled his sweater over his head. "I have to hurry."

Lydia wandered, at loose ends. She took the sketchpad out of the dresser where she'd stowed it. But she opened it and sat, staring at the drawings. She could only imagine the house on the headland. It wouldn't come when she tried to reconcile herself to the idea of building it in another place.

"Working again?"

"You are fast." He'd changed into a charcoal suit that made him formal, less approachable. "Good thing you brought that."

"Habit," he said. "Are you going to be all right?"

"Sure. Josh?"

He looked back.

"We've wasted time these past few days. We need to talk tonight about where we're going to live."

"I'm for that."

She grinned. "Good. Let's decide on our own future after you sort out Luke's."

She watched him drive away. He waved, but he was already in court. For the first time in as long as she could remember, she didn't mind. Their marriage came first. The rest, they'd figure out.

She stared at the sketches for a while longer and then got up to make coffee. While it percolated, she opened the cupboard that hid Evelyn's small TV. As Lydia switched it on, she happened to see Mitch Dawson prowling near the barn.

She reached for the phone.

His right hand was rammed in his coat pocket. He stared at the house. She ducked away from the window. When she rose again, he was on the headland.

She put the phone back, alarms ringing like Christmas bells in her head. He dropped beneath a spiny, leafless maple and slumped to one side, desolation seeping from every pore.

She should call the police. A guy his age didn't always use a gun on other people and his whole body reflected sadness.

"Damn." She watched a few more seconds. He drew something from his right pocket and stared at it intently. Lydia grabbed her coat and eased out of the mudroom door. Hurrying, practically on her toes, she tried not to startle him, but she didn't want to alert him early to her presence.

A few steps behind his back, she cleared her throat. He jumped, but the gun remained unfired. He turned, pointing it at her.

"What do you want?" she asked, trying to steel herself against trembling.

"Revenge. I came for your husband. He's taking my brother to court. Why does he want us in jail?"

She wouldn't look at the gun that shook in his hand. "He's trying to help your brother out of the trouble you got him into."

"You're blaming me?" His voice rose. She pushed her fists into her pockets.

"Face facts, Mitch. You're eighteen years old and you're screwing up the rest of your life. You're in a little trouble now, but if you use that gun, you'll have no life. And why?"

"Because of your do-gooding husband. I know he hates his parents. He hates anyone who isn't a goodie-goodie like him." He stretched his face in a vicious parody of crying. "My baby sister died. My parents are drunks. Feel sorry for me—and oh, look, I'm a big hero."

"No." She almost reminded him it was her fault the police had looked at him and his brother.

"He told my grandmother about this. Was that helpful?" He held up the gun. He glanced at her and then returned his stare to the ocean. "I thought I could get here before he left."

"You'd better be glad you didn't."

"Or?" He lifted the gun again, and his hand still shook as he pointed it at her chest.

She didn't dare speak. He ran his tongue across his lips. He flexed his hand and then took a tight grip again.

Lydia flinched, preparing herself for pain. Nothing came. The gun kept shaking. Finally, Mitch swore at the top of his lungs and the gun dropped to his side.

Now was not the time to say she hadn't believed he'd shoot her.

"So I can't hurt you." He turned the gun toward his belly and she rushed at him, holding off to keep from jostling him. "This might be a good idea," he said.

"Mitch, don't." She had to speak through tears. "A kid like you throwing his life away. You know I just lost a little boy?"

"I'm not little, and I'm not your boy." He rubbed the gun, almost lovingly. "I'm no one's son, and I'm tired of trying to figure out why."

"Why your parents don't seem to want you?"

"Forget about the 'seem.' It doesn't hurt my feelings anymore."

"Which is why you came to shoot my husband, but you've decided to kill yourself?"

"You're not good at crisis counseling."

"Throw that gun in the ocean." She patted her pockets, "because I forgot my phone. I can't call for help. And if you ever come near my husband again, you'll need more than a gun to protect yourself from me."

"Oh, tough chick." He stood. "You know my grandmother called the police? They were coming when I ran out the back. They'll be here soon enough because I told her I was going to take care of Josh Quincy."

"Good. They can take you to get some help."

"This is all the help I need."

He couldn't hide his bravado, or the "Why?" writ large on his face and the tears that pooled in his eyes. He was scared.

The waves, plunging at the cliff, silenced her few steps through the dry, brown grass. Salt slapped her in the face and the wind twisted her hair with gale force.

If only that kid was right and the police were on their way. "Why don't you give me the gun?" she asked.

"Stay away."

Movement, out on the road, caught her eye. Evelyn's car, coming silently to a halt. Lydia nearly stopped breathing.

Desperately, she circled Mitch and he turned with her. Putting Josh's parents behind him. She couldn't wave them off without showing Mitch they were there.

"Give me the gun," she said again. "You heard me tell the police I didn't know if you were one of the kids at the school. I don't want to get you in trouble."

"I'm through with trouble. I just wish I could take Luke with me."

Horror stopped her until she realized he was still talking. He must not be sure he wanted to die.

Behind him, Bart got out of the car. Lydia gritted her teeth.

"Please," she finally managed to say.

"Come to the edge of the cliff with me."

"No." She'd all but yelled, realizing Bart had ducked onto a small ledge that ran along the edge of the cliff.

"Fine." Mitch turned and headed toward the ocean. "Tell my grandma I didn't know what else to do."

"All this over a few pranks?"

"I know what'll happen to me after this. I've threatened you with a gun. I broke into a store for bullets. You think people forget about that?"

"I think Josh could make people think twice about the pain you're in."

"I'm not in any freakin' pain. I'm fed up with my gran and Luke and the cops and my mom, and I don't know what to do anymore."

He turned. At the same time, Bart sprang over the cliff. He ran straight into Mitch. Lydia hit the ground as they did.

No gunshot rang out, but male voices and heavy breathing accompanied a knot of older man and young, rolling toward danger on the edge of the cliff.

Suddenly, a siren pierced the air. It stopped Mitch for a moment. Lydia ran and kicked the gun out of his hand.

"Bitch," he said.

"Are you all right?" Bart asked.

"Are you out of your mind? He could have killed you."

"Or you." Bart held on to the struggling boy, swearing and writhing beneath him. Lydia went over and sat on the kid's feet. His fight began to fade once he couldn't move.

"You don't happen to have rope?" her father-in-law asked, gasping for air.

"What were you thinking, Bart?"

"That I wouldn't let another daughter die."

He brought Lydia almost back to her knees, which applied more pressure to Mitch, who called her a bitch again. She braced a hand on her thigh and leaned over to pat Bart's back. "I am your daughter."

The police veered onto the road where Bart had parked the car. They passed it and soon the men were running through the grass to drag Mitch off the ground.

"Ev called the cops on her cell phone," Bart said, climbing to his feet as Evelyn threw herself at him, hitting him like a bag of wet sand. "The best invention since the wheel. I'm fine, Ev, just fine."

Simon Chambers took over, barking demands. Within seconds, two of his men had cuffed Mitch.

Simon suddenly filled Lydia's vision. "Mrs. Quincy, I see you're all right."

Maybe.

"You're lucky," he said. "You kept yourself under control, and your father-in-law saved your life."

"Lydia." A man stepped out of the group around Simon to croak her name. Josh's voice, cut with fear and nameless agony, drew her.

He searched her body with his eyes and then with his hands. His fingers shook as he traced her arms and legs and finally her stomach and back. "Are you all right?"

She nodded, weakness stealing through her as rage faded away. She couldn't seem to control her own body.

"She's all right, thanks to Bart," Simon said. "You gotta take these kids seriously."

"The gun didn't even go off," Lydia said.

"Dad?" Josh turned to his parents with wonder. "*You* saved Lydia?"

"No." Lydia's voice trembled beneath a heavy load of adrenaline. "He tried to get himself killed."

THE POLICE FINALLY LEFT. Josh followed his parents and Lydia back to the house. They sprawled in the family room. He did that, too.

All the while, sweat soaked him. His head was pounding. He thought his brain might explode. He was about to be sick in front of all of them.

He didn't like being afraid. In fact, it shamed him. He was so furious he wanted to drive back to Hartford without Lydia.

"A kid has a gun, so you go out to chat. How smart was that, Lydia?"

"He's a confused kid."

"He's not me." Josh tried to remember holding her, loving her, needing her. He needed to stop being afraid. He stood, his arms shaking. "I don't want to care this much." He wouldn't risk loving and losing another human being.

"What?" Lydia looked stricken. "When Mitch threatened you, I told him he might as well throw his gun in the ocean because he'd never get through me."

Josh's own cowardice cut him off at the knees. "I'm sorry," he said.

"How about some privacy?" His mother came to her senses and towed his father from the room.

"I'm nothing," Josh said. "You don't need me." *I don't want to be needed.* Not by someone whose life mattered more to him than his own.

"You want to leave me now?" Tears wet Lydia's eyes. "Why now? What did I do?"

"I can't—" Inside, he was fragmented, an unborn boy's father, Lydia's unsatisfactory husband, Clara's failure as a brother. But all those pieces refused to fit together and heal.

"I couldn't just let him shoot himself." She pushed her hands into her hair, despair in the curl of her fingers. "I didn't know if he meant it, but he's so young. Horrible, but young and he feels unloved."

"I love you too much," Josh said.

She stared at him again. "I don't understand you."

"I saw him on the ground and the gun and my dad, and I pictured it another way. What if you had died?"

"I didn't. I'm not even sure the gun was loaded properly. Your dad knocked the hell out of it. I kicked it halfway down the cliff. It never went off."

"I can't face it again."

"Face losing someone? All these years, you've been pushing me away because you're not good at losing people you love?" Lydia looked relieved.

"I can't lose you. Don't you see?" He turned toward the door and escape. "Don't think I can change because I know what's wrong," he said. "I don't want to be here. I don't want to love you like this."

He hit the door, running. He was on the headland before he knew he'd left the house. The grass was crushed and torn where his father and Lydia had wrestled Mitch.

He groaned.

"I don't care what you want."

Josh turned.

Lydia stood behind him, her eyes as bright as rain in a puddle. "You do love me, and you can't stop, can you?"

He couldn't answer.

"I know you want me," she said, though the first hint of doubt entered her voice.

Somehow that hurt more.

He caught her close. "I couldn't get to you at the hospital. They wouldn't let me hold you because you were so hurt. I kept telling myself it was my fault, that you'd leave me. And you almost did. Then, I thought we'd made it."

"We have. You're not going anywhere, because I can't imagine losing you either. We'll make everything okay. It's over now, Josh."

"Over?"

"We know what's wrong."

And despite what he'd said, she thought they could fix it?

She put her arms around him, tentatively.

"I don't want to do this," he said, and yet his arms went around her. He held her so tightly the breath whooshed from her lungs.

She laughed with strange relief. "Josh, we have no choice. We love each other. All the fear we can both feel won't take you away from me. I'm not going away."

He buried his face in her hair. "A man is not supposed to feel like this."

"I don't care what else you feel as long as you love me."

It was a gift. Unconditional love that wasn't ashamed of him because he was a coward. He might not be enough, but the woman he'd love all his life believed he was.

"I will," he said. "I'll love you all my life—until I'm an empty hulk, incapable of feeling."

Lydia cradled his face and brushed her lips across his. "That has to be one of the most unattractive images I've ever faced, but with you, it sounds close enough to forever."

AFTER DINNER, they went to their room. Josh closed the door and locked it. He stripped and slid into bed. Lydia was only a few steps behind him.

He turned off the light and then got up to open the curtains so that moonlight came in. "I still don't know what exactly happened," he said, climbing back into bed.

Naked, she opened her arms to him. They wrapped themselves around each other, arms and legs a perfect fit. How had she lived without his touch?

"Geraldine called the police," she said, "after Mitch threatened you."

"So they were on their way? Simon called me at the courthouse."

She trembled with exhaustion. "You'll help Mitch, won't you, Josh?"

"You realize you're asking me to do the very work that almost split us up?"

"I finally see why you do it. His father abandoned him and his mother prefers some guy to him and his brother. You are a good man who's been in more pain than Mitch Dawson will ever know, and you chose to live. He needs help, from a good man, not jail time." She looked into her husband's shadowed eyes. "And he made me believe when he turned the gun on himself. Even now I don't know if he was serious, but I told Geraldine about it tonight."

"She asked my mom for a therapist's name. I guess she thinks my mother and father know the local psychologists since they still attend AA meetings."

"What about Luke?"

"He explained and the judge believed him. It wasn't hard since the whole courthouse heard the police force was chasing his brother."

"I mean him and Mitch," she said.

"Luke is going to see the counselor, too, but I don't expect he'll let Mitch use him as a punching bag after today. He was humiliated in court. He's not gangster material."

"And what about us? Are we okay?"

"I love you, Lydia. You're my wife—my heart.

My soul is tangled up with yours. You want me even when I'm sure I'm just half a man."

Choked by her own love, she couldn't answer. She looked up at him, and he kissed her cheekbones and her nose, finally her mouth, until her body was clay, longing for his touch.

"I want your time and your babies and my side of your bed for the rest of our lives."

A long time later, when her heart seemed to be struggling for release, he eased back.

"Another thing," he said.

"Uh-huh." She blew her tousled hair out of her eyes. "I'll agree to whatever you ask."

"I'm thinking there's plenty to keep me busy here. If I open my own office, we probably couldn't afford land somewhere else, and we have the headland."

Joy exploded inside Lydia, flashing through her body. Pleasant-painful joy.

"Besides," Josh said, "where could our family be safer? My lunatic father would give his own life to keep us from harm."

Laughing, Lydia held on to him with all her strength. "We are going to make it."

"And you love me."

So they still had pride issues. "I love you," she said against his ear, laughing as he shivered. She took his lobe between her teeth and breathed gently. "I'm dying to show you."

"We have to wait five more days, three hours and fourteen minutes." He tilted her against him, and Lydia lost track of what he was saying.

She wriggled closer, breathing in the delicious scent of his bare chest. "We aren't going to make that," she said.

EPILOGUE

Two years later

"ONCE MORE, Lydia." Dr. Forbes, in mask and gown, sat between her legs, demanding the impossible.

"Lydia," Josh said, "concentrate. We're almost there."

She gathered her strength, pretty certain part of it came from the large hands bracing her shoulders, and then she pushed as hard as she could.

"Wait, wait." Dr. Forbes laughed. A baby screamed.

Not *a* baby. Her baby and Josh's. Their daughter, if the ultrasounds were right. The lights blurred in front of Lydia. The muttering machines took her back to that long-gone day when she'd awakened in another hospital.

"Is she all right?" Lydia asked.

Her infant daughter bellowed with the affront

of any sensible girl being forced from a warm, cozy place into the real world.

"She's fine." Dr. Forbes beckoned Josh, who cut the cord, looking proud, but endearingly bemused.

A nurse examined their daughter and then wrapped her in a pink blanket and passed her to her father. Josh leaned onto the bed and Lydia pressed her cheek to their baby girl's.

The baby stopped screaming to stare at her parents, who couldn't take their eyes off her.

"We still don't have a name," Lydia said. She wanted Clara. Josh wasn't sure his parents were ready.

"We'll agree on something before we take her home." He kissed Lydia and then he kissed their daughter. "It can't be harder than choosing the bedroom furniture."

"That took us more than six months."

"Not everything can change." Josh laughed, cradling the baby between them. "But I won't change again."

"I believe in you," Lydia said.

"Shh. We're not alone."

"I'm hurrying," Dr. Forbes said. "She's a beauty. See if she'll nurse, Lydia."

Josh helped her arrange the hospital gown. Together, they managed to move their rooting daughter to her breast. The baby took over from there.

"She's starving." The last nurse in the room managed to tidy up the bed, and then she pulled hangings around it. Dr. Forbes pushed his stool back.

Lydia watched her daughter, awestruck. "How did she know how to do that?"

Dr. Forbes and the nurse laughed. "Call if you need us," the doctor said. "We'll be back in a while. Have a nice visit, and I'll hold off Evelyn and Bart as long as I can." He peeled off his gloves and planted his hands on his hips. "You make a fine family."

After they were alone, Josh helped Lydia switch the baby to her other breast, and then he lay down beside them.

"I can't help thinking about our other baby," Lydia said, unsurprised to find that this moment, so laced with happiness could hold a pinch of grief for her lost son.

"He's on my mind." Josh laid his palm against the baby's head. His hand completely swallowed her. "But she deserves all our love, and it wouldn't be fair to let the past make her future bitter." He looked up. "The son we didn't get to know will always have a place in our family, but we have to love her without holding back."

Lydia cuddled the baby closer, smiling as she

uttered the faintest grunt. "I knew I'd love her. I thought it would be all sweet and beautiful." She rubbed her daughter's leg. "But when I look at her, I'd do anything—I feel it from so deep I don't know where it starts. It's savage. I only felt grief like that before."

He tucked a blanket around Lydia, his hand lingering in the loving touch she anticipated every lucky day of her life. "It's different this time. She's in our arms. We're going to take her home to a house you designed just for us. She's going to live and grow up in a town where everyone will look out for her." He smiled, as humbled as Lydia. "I wouldn't have believed this could happen two years ago, but I see the two of you, and I know I'll never wonder where home is again."

Their daughter had fallen asleep. Over her head, Lydia kissed her husband, gently nibbling his whiskered chin.

She snuggled with her daughter and tangled her legs with Josh's, tired, but tranquil. She no longer knew fear. When his clients got out of hand, they were just part of life. She and Josh protected each other and carried on with living, and now they had this living sign of their love, their infant girl.

"I wish we could all sleep like this for a little

while, but any second your parents are going to bust down that door."

Josh slid his hand around her nape and kissed her forehead, his mouth curved in a smile. "We'll pretend we don't notice them."

HARLEQUIN®

Super Romance

SWEET MERCY

by *Jean Brashear*

RITA® Award-nominated author!
HSR #1339

Once, Gamble Smith had everything—and
then the love of his life decided, against
medical advice, to have his child. Now he is a
man lost in grief. Jezebel Hart can heal him.
But she carries a secret she wants to share—one
she knows Gamble isn't ready to hear, one
that could destroy what the two of them have
together.

On sale April 2006

Available wherever Harlequin books are sold!

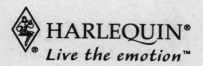

HARLEQUIN®
® *Live the emotion™*

HARLEQUIN®

Super Romance

UNEXPECTED COMPLICATION

by *Amy Knupp*

HSR #1342

A brand-new Superromance author
makes her debut in 2006!

Carey Langford is going to have a baby. Too
bad the father's a louse, and she has to do this
alone. Fortunately, she has the support of her
best friend, Devin Colyer. If only Devin could
accept the child's paternity and admit his true
feelings for Carey....

On sale April 2006
Available wherever Harlequin books are sold!

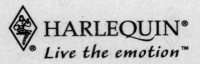

HARLEQUIN®
Live the emotion™

You're never too old to sneak out at night

BJ thinks her younger sister, Iris, needs a love interest. So she does what any mature woman would do and organizes an Over-Fifty Singles Night. When her matchmaking backfires it turns out to be the best thing either of them could have hoped for.

Over 50's Singles Night

by Ellyn Bache

Available April 2006
TheNextNovel.com

HN37

HARLEQUIN®
NExt™

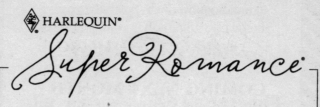

OVER HIS HEAD

by Carolyn McSparren

HSR #1343

Single Father: He's a man on his own, trying
to raise his children. Sometimes he gets things
right. Sometimes he needs a little help....

Tim Wainwright may be a professional
educator, but since his wife died he
hasn't had a clue how to handle his own
children. Ironically, even Tim's new neighbor,
Nancy Mayfield—a vet tech who prefers
animals to people—seems to understand his
kids better than he does.

On sale April 2006
Available wherever Harlequin books are sold!

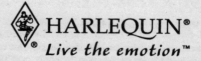

HARLEQUIN®
Live the emotion™

HARLEQUIN®
Super Romance

COMING NEXT MONTH